THE NEXT FILES
DOUBLE PUZZLER

LANG SUYAR

And

BLOOD OF THE AZTECS

by

G L Keady

ALSO BY
G L Keady

DREAMRAIDERS
SONS OF STEEL
CHANNELING BO
THE INCARNATE

Axis Stone Mysteries

SUICIDE BLONDE
LEG MAN
SMUGGLER'S HOLE
HORSE ARM CASE
GOD'S DOOR
THE SACRED THREE
THE GIRL WITH THE LUNATIC FRINGE
CAT STREET
THE ZIGGY STARDUST DEAD RINGER

Sons of Steel Saga

FUTURES END
CYBERWARS
DARK ENERGY
BLOCKCHAIN
AL AND THE ID
TABLETS OF DESTINIES
DOMINION
ALL THE TIME IN THE WORLD

The Next Files

EIGHT DRAGONS
MIN MIN

Big Island Publishing
PO Box 3027, Tuross Head, 2537, NSW, Australia
www.bigislandpublishing.au

ISBN:
E-book: 9780975633069
Print: 9780975633076

Edited by: Canon Doyle
Cover design: Brandon Evans-Keady

TABLE OF CONTENTS

BLOOD OF THE AZTECS

CHAPTER ONE

The thatched-roof hut, perched on stilts to escape Sabah's heavy seasonal rains, was home to a family of six. They sat on the floor inside, finishing their dinner. That night, a wild wind stormed through, rattling the hut and howling like a thousand wolves.

Lani, eighteen and five months pregnant, felt sleepy. After drinking a cup of water, she stood up, gave her parents a goodnight kiss, and walked to her bedroom. Being the eldest, she had her own small room.

Outside, the wind was a force to reckon with, bending the coconut palms surrounding the hut and whisking mist through the trees, enveloping the hut. The night was pitch black, with only the full moon occasionally breaking through the storm clouds to cast eerie shadows. It was the kind of night that made the superstitious villagers stay locked up tight in their homes.

Clawed hands parted the hut's thatch, allowing the candlelight below to reveal Lani on a woven bed. Dressed in shorts and a loose white T-shirt, she lifted the garment to tenderly touch her pregnant belly. A solitary tear meandered down her cheek, a silent testament to her affection. The candle's flicker dwindled as the wick burned out, plunging the room into darkness just as Lani's eyes closed, surrendering to sleep.

Malevolent yellow eyes, with elongated, cat-like pupils, peered down at Lani, filled with a sinister hunger. The Lang Suyar, sniffing the air like a hound, detected the foetus within Lani. It opened its mouth, revealing rows of sharp teeth, and extended its serpentine tongue through the thatch. The tongue slithered downward, inching towards Lani's exposed belly. Amidst the howling wind, lightning illuminated the room, and a thunderclap shook the hut, yet Lani remained asleep, oblivious to the ghastly appendage nearing her.

A brighter lightning flash, followed by an even more thunderous clap—Lani jolted upright, she screamed in terror, a sound that echoed through the night, before collapsing back onto her bed, unconscious.

Friday nights were always buzzing at the Friend in Hand Pub, but this particular evening saw an even larger crowd. The reason? The Electric Roses, an all-girl teenage band, were playing. Despite their debut record 'Take Me' rocketing to the top of the charts, they still cherished these intimate pub gigs, staying connected with their fans.

Jax elbowed her way to the bar, ordering a beer. She was on the lookout for her work partner, Doc Lee. His unique blend of Filipino and Chinese heritage, combined with his tall, handsome stature, usually made him easy to spot in a crowd. But tonight, with everyone dancing and swaying to the music, finding him was like searching for a needle in a haystack.

The band's lead singer, a slim figure with long brown hair, commanded the stage. Clad in a black T-shirt adorned with a red, battery-powered rose that pulsed to the rhythm, her barefooted stance and tattooed arms gave her a rough, edgy look. Yet, her voice was pure magic, rumoured to span four octaves. As one song ended, the pub fell into a hush of anticipation. The lights dimmed, a spotlight enveloped her, and as she closed her eyes, the crowd erupted in cheers. They knew what was next. With a confident air, she launched into their hit song 'Take Me.'

> When I close my eyes ... take me....
> Lately, I've been dreaming of
> All the things I'd love to do, with you
> Take my hand and we'll go walking, aha
> High above the clouds just me and you

Lights blazed across the stage, and a dozen rotating spotlights swept through the audience with beams of white light, slicing through the darkness like a scythe.

> We'll fly so high into the night sky
> Tears of ice will fill our eyes
> We look down and see tomorrow
> And we'll make believe that
> everything's all right...

> Maybe I am guilty of
> Building castles in the air
> But dreams alone can colour darkness, aha
> A light shining bright will guide us there...

> We'll fly so high into the night sky
> Tears of ice will fill our eyes
> We'll look down and see tomorrow
> and make believe that
> everything's all right...

The lead singer reached into the mosh pit, grabbing a guy's hand and yanking him up onto the stage. Jax wasn't shocked to see it was Doc. He jumped right into the chorus, jamming with the singer as if they were an item.

> We'll fly so high into the night sky
> Tears of ice will fill our eyes
> We'll look down and see tomorrow
> and make believe that
> everything's all right...

Jax found herself swept up in the moment, dancing and singing along. The tune was just too catchy.

> Introduce me to a higher plane
> Take me, teach me something new, ahaha
> I will give my love - in return
> Lead the way I'll come with you...

As the last chorus hit its peak, the whole audience joined in, singing their hearts out.

> Take me around the world, oh yeah
> Make my senses swirl, oh yeah
> I wanna feel your love inside me
> Take me, take me, take me…
> Oh yeah, yeah, yeah, yeah
> Oh yeah…!

> Take me around the world, oh yeah!
> Make my senses swirl, oh yeah!
> I wanna feel your love inside me
> Take me, take me, take me…
> Yeah, yeah, yeah, yeah, yeah … Oh yeah…

The song reached a dramatic musical climax and then, boom—the stage lights snapped off. By the time the house lights came back on, the band had vanished.

Jax thought Doc had disappeared backstage with the band, but suddenly, there he was, weaving through the crowd towards her. Jax grabbed a couple of beers from the bar, and as she turned around, Doc was right there. She handed him his drink.

"Looks like you could use this," she said, clinking her glass against his. "Cheers, big ears."

"Hey, I'll have you know, I get loads of compliments on these ears," Doc shot back with a smirk. "All the better to hear you with, little girl."

"Cut the fairy tale gags, they weird me out. So, what's with the sudden stage debut?" Jax asked, a twinkle of jealousy in her eyes.

"Renee, the lead singer, thinks I'm eye candy," Doc grinned.

Jax rolled her eyes. "Well, not everyone's got great taste, do they?"

As the place started to empty, a few people recognised Doc from his gigs, nodding or waving at him.

"Look at you, Mr Rock Star. Soon you'll be signing autographs."

"Jax, get with the times. It's all about selfies now," Doc laughed. "But seriously, what brings you here tonight? You didn't just come for the music."

Jax tried to brush it off, but Doc cut in. "Come on, Jax, spill it."

"Okay, okay..." she sighed. "We've got an early flight to Kuala Lumpur, then connecting to Kota Kinabalu in Sabah."

CHAPTER TWO

Doc was buzzed by the sleek, modern look of Kota Kinabalu International Airport. He'd pictured something way less fancy. Jax, on the other hand, wasn't surprised. She'd been to Kota before on a family diving trip when she was younger.

As they stepped out into the arrivals, a driver was already there, holding up a 'NewsLine' sign. Jax introduced themselves and followed him to the car, ready to head to their next stop.

Walking out of the airport, they got hit by the humid tropical air, so different from Sydney's cool autumn vibe. The city had its own unique buzz.

During the air-conditioned drive, Jax struck up a conversation with the driver. Turns out, he worked for the owner of Hunto Pulp Mill. Apparently, the owner was buddies with NewsLine and had offered them a lift.

Doc was totally caught up in the scenery. The lush rainforests and the jagged skyline of Mount Kinabalu in the distance were just amazing. Soon, they were cruising through the narrow streets of Lobong-Lobong village. The busy market square made them slow down.

Doc, catching the locals' curious looks, asked the driver, "Why are they looking at us like we're vampires or something?"

The driver laughed, "In this part of Malaysia, magic and superstition are part of life, sir. There've been some Lang Suyar attacks lately, so people are a bit jittery."

"The Lang Suyar, that's the flying witch that preys on unborn babies, right?" Jax chimed in.

"Yes, ma'am. The Lang Suyar is feared. The attacks have left many grieving and scared."

A few minutes later, the car swung into a long driveway lined with neat gardens. At the end, a huge, white, three-storey colonial mansion loomed. It was obvious to both Doc and Jax: the owner was rolling in it.

They were greeted at the front steps by a steward who led them through the impressive mansion to a patio beside a swimming pool. There, a small man in a white suit introduced himself as Mr Hantu, the owner of the mansion and the Hantu Pulp Mill. As they settled in for morning tea in a setting that looked like something from a posh magazine, Jax brought up the Lang Suyar.

"I used to think all this was mumbo jumbo until my daughter, Dina, was attacked," Hantu confessed.

Jax and Doc exchanged looks. "So you're the one who contacted Des Carter at NewsLine for us to investigate?" Jax asked.

"Yes, but I expected someone older, not teenage cub reporters. When he mentioned de Ville, I thought of Henry."

"Mr Hantu, my father disappeared in 2017. And for your information, we're not just cub reporters."

After Hantu's confession, the air felt heavy. Doc shifted the conversation. "When did Dina get attacked?"

"A few days back. I was at the pulp mill."

"Where's the mill?"

"On the Kota Belud River, a half-hour from here."

They had gone past the river on their way to the mansion. Jax, getting fed up with Hantu's attitude, pressed on, "Can we see Dina?"

Hantu looked uneasy but eventually agreed, with one condition. "But you'll keep our name out of your story."

"Understood," Jax replied, her tone icy.

After a quick chat with the steward, Hantu had them follow a maid named Rosa upstairs. As they went up, Doc asked, "Was Mr Hantu aware that Dina was pregnant?"

"No, sir," the maid answered, a bit uneasy.

"Did you see the Lang Suyar?" Jax asked next.

"No, miss."

"So, he only found out about the pregnancy after the alleged attack?" Doc checked.

Rosa looked confused by the word 'alleged', so Jax broke it down for her.

"Yes, sir found out then."

"I bet that shook him up," Doc whispered to Jax as they walked into Dina's room.

Dina, a pretty seventeen-year-old, was propped up in bed, glued to her phone. Jax gently drew out Dina's story, while Doc quietly chatted with Rosa about her take on the incident. Dina was clearly upset after talking to Jax. Jax patiently held her hand, giving her time to settle down, then asked Doc to step out for a bit so she could check on Dina privately.

After a while, Jax called Doc and Rosa back in. Rosa helped get Dina comfortable, and Jax gave her a reassuring kiss on the cheek before they all left the room.

Outside, Rosa paused and then shared something with Jax in a low voice, "Miss, this is the third attack in as many weeks. The villagers, and I too, think the Lang Suyar is a woman named Esmerelda Kucing. She moved into a place at the top of the Kota Belud river a few months back."

On their way back to Kota, Jax and Doc reviewed everything they'd picked up. Jax didn't spot any clear signs of an attack on Dina, but what Rosa said about Esmerelda Kucing really got them thinking. Jax figured their next move should be to visit Esmerelda's place. They decided to book a room in a Kota hotel and rent their own car for the investigation. They had a hunch that Hantu's driver might be more than just a driver—maybe even a spy.

On their way in a rental car to visit Esmerelda Kucing, Doc was driving with Jax next to him, navigating. They covered the first twenty kilometres towards Mount Kinabalu and the upper reaches of the Kota Belud River quickly on the surfaced road. But the journey to Esmerelda's house required a detour onto a narrow, bumpy track through dense tropical rainforest. As they neared their destination, Jax, while trying to read aloud from a book on Malay folklore, warned Doc about the potential dangers of encountering a Lang Suyar. "In its human form, a Lang Suyar can be incredibly beautiful and deceptive," she explained. "Just remember, inside she's a horrible monster."

"It's just superstitious garbage," Doc dismissed her concerns.

Jax quipped back, "Keep thinking like that, and you'll lose your underwear."

Doc smiled smugly, "I don't wear any underwear."

Jax made a face, "That's it, never mention your underwear or lack thereof to me again."

They arrived at a clearing where an unexpectedly charming log cabin stood. "Well, that I didn't expect," Doc remarked as they got out of the car.

The front door was surrounded by peculiar charms and trinkets. Jax's eyebrow raised in Doc's direction—for her, these were clear signs of witchcraft. As they approached the porch, a curtain moved slightly, and they saw a shadowy figure peeking at them. Doc, trailing behind Jax, let out a "Boo!" startling her. She turned and playfully punched him in the bicep. Their light mood got a jolt when the front door creaked open just enough for a black cat to sneak out, glaring at them with a growl.

Jax took a careful step back, knowing all about the link between a Lang Suyar and her familiar, a cat. The door then swung open more, showing a stunning lady in her mid-twenties with flowing black hair. She had bare feet sticking out from under a long, dark green caftan. Doc seemed pretty taken with her, but Jax was more focused on her unusually long nails.

"Hello. We're looking for Miss Kucing," Doc said, sounding pretty friendly.

"I am she," she answered back in English with an accent, sounding sweet and kind of inviting.

"I'm Doc Lee, and this is my associate Jax de Ville. We're conducting an investigation and have some questions for you," Doc introduced them.

Jax rolled her eyes at Doc—his crush on Esmerelda was pretty obvious.

"Please, come into my home. Call me Esmerelda," the woman said, leading them inside.

The place was dark, filled with stuffed animals and weird symbols—total witchcraft vibes for Jax. Esmerelda got them to sit in the lounge, pulled back a curtain for some light, and then sat down across from them.

"Your home is very interesting. Are you originally from Lobong-Lobong?" Doc asked.

"No, I moved here from Kota Kinabalu six months ago. I inherited this house from my uncle," Esmerelda shared.

"I'm sorry to hear about your uncle," Doc said sympathetically.

Jax didn't beat around the bush, "Are you aware that the villagers accuse you of being a Lang Suyar?"

"Yes, I've been dealing with that since I came here. It's common for newcomers, especially lone women, to be suspected. But the truth is I'm being targeted by Mr Hantu, the owner of the Hantu Pulp Mill," Esmerelda opened up.

"Why would he do that?" Doc inquired.

"He wanted this property because it includes the source of the Kota Belud River, which is vital for his paper mill. My uncle was a hermit, and Hantu didn't expect him to have a niece. So, he concocted the Lang Suyar story to scare me off," she explained.

"And the three babies' deaths in the village?" Jax pressed.

"They were just a weird coincidence. The Lang Suyar story probably just covered up what I think were illegal abortions," Esmerelda guessed.

Jax was intrigued but not convinced, while Doc seemed to see the logic in Esmerelda's explanation.

CHAPTER THREE

On their way back to the hotel, Jax and Doc were deep into their chat, trying to piece together what they thought had happened. They both knew they needed to talk to the other two victims to really figure things out. So, they headed off to the small village of Lobong-Lobong.

About half an hour later, Jax hopped out of the car in the village square to ask a policeman how to get to Lani's house. The policeman wasn't great with English, so it was a bit of a struggle for Jax to understand his directions.

While she was gone, Doc, sitting in the car with his cool shades and rocker T-shirt, caught the eye of some local girls. They seemed to think he was some kind of movie star. He gave them a big smile, and they all burst out laughing.

When Jax got back to the car, she saw Doc and the girls and gave him a look that said, "Really, again?" Their joke about his flirting was always good for a laugh. Doc waved goodbye to his 'fans' and Jax pointed him down a muddy track through the village.

Driving through a cloud of smoke from a fire someone had lit at the roadside, they ended up in a poorer part of the village. Jax pointed to a hut and Doc parked out front. As they walked up to the front door, it opened up and there stood this old, wrinkly lady. To Doc, she was like something straight out of a fairy tale. He stayed back a bit, letting Jax lead the way.

The woman didn't speak any English, but she called over a young boy who was just as starstruck by Doc as the girls had been.

"We're here to talk to Lani. Is she your sister?" Jax asked the boy.

His gap-toothed smile grew wider. "Yeah, who are you guys?"

"I'm Jax, and this is Doc," she introduced them.

"He's a movie star!" the boy blurted out excitedly.

Jax laughed. "He wishes. What's your name?"

"I'm Akham, it means 'strong,'" he declared, showing off his muscles. "Lani is my sister, and that's my grandma, Bunga. She's 98. 'Bunga' means 'flower.' What about 'Jax'? What does that mean?"

"God is gracious," Jax answered.

Akham looked a bit confused, then waved them in. "Lani's in bed, she's not well."

Inside, Bunga signalled for Doc to sit in a wicker chair, suggesting he wait there, while Jax was to see Lani. Doc, grateful for a can of Coke in the sweltering heat, decided to wait outside the cramped hut. Bunga went with Jax and Akham to Lani's small bedroom.

Lani looked really unwell, pale and frail. Jax gently asked, "Lani, can you tell me what happened?" Lani didn't answer, so Jax had to rely on Akham to talk to Bunga.

Akham translated Jax's question, and Bunga spoke for Lani. "Grandma says Lani was attacked by the Lang Suyar," Akham said. "It can change into animals, like a huge black dog, a hell-hound. It has a bird inside that lets it fly. It can smell an unborn baby, even before the mum knows. It sneaks into dreams and scares people in their sleep. It came while Lani was asleep."

Bunga then approached Lani, pulling back the bedcovers and lifting her T-shirt. Jax saw bruises and wounds around Lani's navel. Bunga pointed at the mark, speaking intensely. "The Lang Suyar was on the roof. It lowered its tongue and took the baby. Look at the mark," Akham translated.

Jax noticed tears on Lani's cheeks. She gently kissed her on the cheek before leaving the room.

Outside, Doc was playing soccer with a group of local boys. As the sun started setting, the boys, almost like they had a shared signal, quickly ran off to their homes, leaving Doc standing there holding the ball. He paused, a little confused, trying to figure out why they'd all suddenly left him there alone.

Back at the car, Jax got in, with Doc following. Inside, she shared her observations. "The kids ran off like that because they're scared of the Lang Suyar. They think it comes out at night."

Doc fired up the car, his voice showing some scepticism. "I think you're getting too wrapped up in this local superstition."

It was dark when Jax and Doc got back to their hotel. As they parked, the sound of thunder rumbled through the car park. Walking towards the lift, Doc noted the change in the weather. "Feels like the pressure and humidity's changing with this storm rolling in."

Jax nodded in agreement. "They get some pretty wild storms here. I remember this one time, I was here with my parents. They were diving off a boat. Suddenly, this huge storm came out of nowhere. The crew wanted to head back to Kota, but they couldn't contact my folks underwater."

As Doc pressed the button for the elevator, he asked, "So what happened?"

Jax's voice tensed up a bit. "It was scary. The storm hit us hard—lightning, thunder, rain like needles. The sea got really rough, and everyone was freaking out. Then, out of nowhere, my parents popped up, and we had to race back to Kota. It was a wild ride, like sailing through hell itself ... but we made it."

Stepping into the lift, Doc remarked, "Getting caught in a storm at sea is no joke."

"It's even worse during a typhoon in the Philippines," Jax added seriously. "Once, in Makati, in our flat, Tilly, Digger, and I were alone; our parents were away. This massive typhoon was coming. The sky turned this dark, purple colour with crazy lightning. Our whole building was shaking from the wind. I remember seeing a sheet of metal fly past our window on the 25th floor, and then a bird, just swept away by the storm. Tilly tried to make a joke about the bird breaking the sound barrier. It lightened the mood a bit."

Doc responded, "A flying sheet of metal up that high? That's seriously dangerous."

Jax went on, "When the rain started, it was like a flood. The streets filled up with water in no time flat. I heard these three kids got sucked down a drain. It was a tragedy. After a typhoon like that, the Filipinos often have to start over from scratch."

The lift doors opened to their floor. "Sounds like storms aren't really your thing," Doc figured out.

"You could say that," Jax agreed, stopping at her room door. "How about breakfast in the coffee shop at 7?"

"Goodnight," Doc said, half-joking. "If the storm gets too much, just give me a shout."

Jax replied with a smirk, "You've got a better chance of winning the lottery, mate."

Doc was jolted awake by the howling wind outside. A tree branch lashed against his window with a violent force. Annoyed, he got up and yanked the curtain open. To his horror, a grotesque face snarled back at him from the other side of the glass!

In an instant, the creature smashed through the window, its clawed fingers lunging for his throat. As they tightened, choking him, Doc struggled desperately. Rain and wind whipped into the room through the shattered window, turning the fight into a chaotic battle. He managed to drag the monster fully inside, grappling fiercely. With a swift move, Doc slipped his fingers under the creature's claws, freeing himself from its deadly grip. He then unleashed a flurry of martial arts strikes, sending the creature stumbling backward onto the floor.

The wind howled, the curtain flapping wildly like ghostly arms in the storm. As the creature struggled to rise, it transformed into Jax! Doc froze, his fist poised for a fatal strike, his mind racing, "Is that her?" But his hesitation was costly. The creature lunged again, its sharp nails slashing his face, leaving deep, agonizing gouges.

Then, suddenly, he sat up in bed, drenched in sweat, heart pounding. It had all been a nightmare. He glanced at the window—it was intact. Unbeknownst to him, the Lang Suyar lurked outside, perched in the tree. It had invaded his dreams, bringing the terror of the night to life. Silently, it took flight, disappearing into the darkness.

CHAPTER FOUR

"It felt so real ... I'm serious, I thought it actually happened. Totally freaked me out," Doc confessed to Jax, who was sitting across from him at the breakfast table in the hotel coffee shop.

Jax peered at him over her coffee cup, noting his unusually disturbed demeanour. With a hint of sarcasm, she remarked, "I think you're getting a little too caught up in this local superstition."

Doc got her sarcasm but remained unsettled, taking a sip of his coffee to compose himself. "We should talk to the doctor who treated these girls. Getting the blood samples analysed could give us some answers."

Jax sensed that her sarcastic comment hadn't lightened the mood as intended; Doc's nightmare had genuinely shaken him. "I agree, though I still think there's something supernatural about Lani's miscarriage."

"We'll have to agree to disagree on that," he replied, finishing his coffee and standing up. "Let's get to it."

Later that morning, Jax and Doc managed to track down Dr Ong, the doctor who had treated the victims. He was a middle-aged Chinese Malay guy, not very tall, but really professional and helpful. He told them that he'd taken blood samples from each of the girls as part of the usual process and had sent them off to Kuala Lumpur for tests. He mentioned that they should be getting the results back pretty soon.

"What's your take on the cause of these miscarriages, doctor?" Doc inquired.

Dr Ong didn't beat around the bush. "In Mari and Lani's cases, it's clear it was a Lang Suyar attack. But with Dina Hantu, it was an abortion."

Jax leaned in, curious. "Could you explain a bit more, Doctor?"

"For Mari and Lani, the foetus was removed through the navel. That wasn't the case with Dina Hantu."

"And the missing remains in all three cases?" Doc followed up.

Dr Ong leaned back, looking serious. "Only the girls themselves can really tell you that. In the Lang Suyar attacks, they would have been out cold, and the creature would have taken the unborn."

As they were about to leave his office, Dr Ong promised he'd let them know the blood test results as soon as he got them. Just then, the receptionist spoke urgently in Bahasa. Jax and Doc exchanged a look, sensing trouble.

Dr Ong turned to them, his face solemn. "There was another attack last night."

In Li's bedroom, Doc and Jax stood quietly as Dr Ong attended to the shivering girl, her body wrapped in a sheet, her forehead glistening with sweat.

"She's got a fever," Jax whispered to Doc, her eyes scanning the room and pausing at the ceiling. "Look, there's a hole in the thatch. That's how the Lang Suyar would have got to her."

Once Dr Ong had finished his examination, he guided them back downstairs. In the living room, he began to explain, "This case is identical to Dina Hantu's," but was suddenly interrupted by a commotion at the door.

Li's parents were struggling to hold back Li's boyfriend, who was desperately trying to see her. The young man lashed out at Li's father. Doc quickly intervened, escorting the distraught boyfriend outside.

The young man, now outside, squared up to Doc, ready to fight. A crowd began to gather, sensing a confrontation. Jax followed, shouting to the young man, "Don't do it, he'll take you down."

Doc's reaction was quick and firm—a swift slap that sent the boy stumbling back, more his pride hurt than anything else. Right then, Dr Ong came outside, joining the tense scene.

"The villagers are all worked up over this Lang Suyar stuff, but let's be real, this was a botched illegal abortion," Dr Ong said, getting straight to the point. "Right now, our top priority is making sure Li doesn't get an infection."

Jax was just getting to her hotel room when she heard her phone ring from inside. She rushed in and picked up just in time. It was Dr Ong's receptionist; the results from the blood tests were back. The receptionist had something surprising to report: there were traces of methyl mercury in the samples.

Doc, standing in the doorway, watched Jax closely as she was on the phone. After she hung up, she filled him in. Doc started pacing the room, thinking hard. Then he suddenly stopped and turned to Jax, a lightbulb moment hitting him.

"Of course, of course," he burst out, a theory forming. "Methyl mercury, used in paper production, banned in most places, including Malaysia. We should check out the pulp mill. Maybe they're using it illegally and polluting the water."

Jax agreed, getting what he was getting at. "That makes sense. We'll have to sneak in there tonight, when it's dark."

With nightfall still hours away, Jax and Doc decided to split their efforts. Jax planned to confront Esmerelda with new questions, while Doc set out to obtain a layout of the pulp mill and an assay of the river water from the mayor's office.

Before parting, Doc asked Jax, "Why go after Esmerelda now, especially with this new clue?"

"It's Friday," Jax answered.

Doc gave her a confused look. "And?"

"On Fridays, if you catch your reflection in a Lang Suyar's eyes, it appears inverted. I need to check if Esmerelda is the Lang Suyar."

Doc left, chuckling to himself, more convinced than ever that the Lang Suyar was just a myth.

Exiting the rental car, Jax felt a rush of both resolve and nervousness. She looked at the orange in her hand, which, according to the legends she'd read up on, was a protection against the Lang Suyar. She opened the trunk, took out a broom—another piece of folklore supposed to keep away supernatural creatures—and, with these items in hand, walked confidently towards Esmerelda's house.

Reaching the porch, Jax placed the broom across the entrance, remembering the belief that a Lang Suyar couldn't cross over it. She grabbed a handful of dirt, another supposed magical shield. Holding the earth in one hand and the orange in the other, she knocked on the door. It opened slowly with a creak, adding to the eerie feel of the place. When she didn't get an answer to her calls, "Esmerelda, are you there? Esmerelda?" Jax cautiously stepped inside.

The creaking floorboards sent chills through her. The dark room was filled with stuffed animals, their lifeless glass eyes seeming to follow her every move. She moved slowly, the floor groaning with each step.

Suddenly, there was a sharp hiss and yowl. Jax had stepped on a black cat's tail. Her heart racing, she quickly apologised to the scared cat. She glanced to the side and caught her own reflection in a mirror, startling herself. Then, a noise from the other direction made her turn sharply. Esmerelda burst out of the shadows, screaming, holding a meat cleaver.

"Stop Esmerelda, it's Jax!" Jax yelled, throwing up her hands to protect herself, the earth spilling from her grip and the orange dropping to the floor.

Esmerelda stopped, cleaver still in the air. Jax, still trembling, begged, "Please, put it down."

To Jax's shock, Esmerelda suddenly started crying. Trying to calm her down, Jax said, "I'm sorry … I'm sorry, I must have frightened you…"

Esmerelda cried harder. "It's not that … I got a death threat from someone in the village."

Jax began to understand why Esmerelda was so scared. She still wanted to check Esmerelda against the folklore. "Maybe it's from the boyfriend of the girl who was attacked last night. Let's go outside, I need to get my phone and call the cops," she suggested, guiding her towards the door.

Outside, Jax stopped and waited for Esmerelda to come out too, but Esmerelda just stayed in the doorway, her head down, not moving an inch. Worried, Jax stepped closer. "Esmerelda?" she asked softly.

Esmerelda finally looked up, and Jax saw she was wearing sunglasses. Jax felt a pang of disappointment; she wouldn't be able to see her reflection in Esmerelda's eyes, which was a key part of her plan. Despite trying to get Esmerelda to step over the threshold, the woman wouldn't budge, staying put right where she was.

After deciding it was a lost cause, Jax went back to her car to get her phone. She called the police to report the threat, mentioning she thought it might be Ti's boyfriend. After hanging up, she went back to Esmerelda. "You should be fine now. The police will have a word with him," she reassured her.

Esmerelda's disbelief and frustration were evident. "The police? They're just like everyone else," she said, her eyes fixed on the broom lying on the ground. Abruptly, she turned, retreated inside her house, and slammed the door.

But the door swung open again seconds later, and the orange Jax had earlier rolled out onto the porch. Shockingly, it looked withered, as if it had aged weeks in mere moments. The door then slammed shut once more, leaving Jax to process the bizarre and unsettling turn of events.

Jax felt a bit defeated and still had so many questions. She picked up the broom and walked back to her car, ready to head back to the hotel.

CHAPTER
FIVE

At 10 PM, the Hantu Pulp Mill cast a sinister shadow, its dark, hulking structure dominating the night. Doc and Jax moved stealthily along the towering wire fence enclosing the factory, each step deliberate and silent in the looming darkness. The only source of light was a lone bulb hanging over the main gate, near a CCTV camera they meticulously avoided.

Spotting a side gate, Doc, with Jax keeping a sharp lookout for any guards, skilfully manipulated the lock. Jax was barely containing her surprise as the gate silently swung open, allowing them a discreet entry. But then, she caught the sound of approaching footsteps and saw a security guard with a ferocious pit bull in tow.

"Doc!" she hissed urgently.

Doc whirled around, instantly sizing up the threat. "Go, Jax, run!" he ordered. Hesitation flickered in Jax's eyes, but at Doc's insistent, "Run! Damn it!" she bolted, sprinting into the shadows.

The guard was blowing his whistle, a clear call for reinforcements. Doc braced himself as the pit bull launched itself at him, a snarling mass of fury. He deflected the attack with a powerful Kung Fu kick, sending the animal yelping into the fence.

Then it was the guard's turn, coming at Doc with a tonfa, a heavy baton used by police. Doc expertly evaded the attack, then countered with a swift and precise knee strike, leaving the guard winded. A quick karate chop to the neck, and the guard crumpled to the ground, unconscious.

Meanwhile, Jax was now the target of the enraged pit bull. Having briefly paused at the end of the fence to catch her breath, she was alerted by Doc's shout, "Jax, the dog!" Whirling around, she saw the pit bull barrelling towards her. Desperate, she clambered onto some oversized PVC pipes, barely gaining height but close to the fence. The sharp razor wire atop the fence glinted menacingly in the faint light. In a split-second decision, she ripped off her T-shirt and flung it over the wire, then, with the pit bull snapping viciously below, made a daring leap for the fence, grasping the now-covered razor wire.

The pit bull backed away, then lunged forward with a mighty leap, managing to sink its teeth into Jax's jeans. Jax tried to climb higher, but the dog's grip was like a dead weight. Just then, Doc arrived, T-baton in hand, and struck the dog on the head, rendering it unconscious. Despite being knocked out, the dog's jaws remained clamped onto Jax's jeans.

"Get your jeans off," Doc suggested.

"No way!" Jax retorted.

"Why not?"

"Because … I'm not wearing any underwear, okay?"

Doc paused, arms crossed, struggling to hold back a laugh. "Thought we were avoiding underwear talk."

Eventually, the jean leg tore, and the dog fell to the ground. Jax, now in just her bra and jeans, finally made it over the wire.

"Leave your shirt. I'll grab it," Doc said, quickly scaling the fence before the dog could recover.

They tracked the large pipes down to the river. While collecting water samples, Jax noticed another pipe upstream, churning the water into foam. She pushed through some bushes to take a sample from that spot.

There, she spotted something tangled on a tree branch in the water. It was a body, floating face down. She called Doc over, and together they pulled it ashore. Turning the body over, they both gasped in shock. Even with the face half-eaten, they could tell—it was Esmeralda.

Cindy, a young village girl, was quickly making her way through the cemetery, a common shortcut to Lobong-Lobong village. The cemetery was usually avoided at night, with its dark corners and the spooky sounds of the wind. As she moved along the path, she noticed a figure draped in a dark green cloak walking towards her.

They passed by each other without any trouble, but then the cloaked figure suddenly stopped and sniffed the air, moving like a hunter that had picked up a scent. Unbeknownst to Cindy, its eyes were a chilling yellow, glowing in the darkness, somehow aware of her pregnancy, a fact Cindy didn't even know herself.

Feeling a sudden cold fear, Cindy sped up, but the figure turned and started following her, floating just off the ground. Sensing something was terribly wrong, Cindy stopped. She dug into her bag and pulled out a string of glass beads, a talisman meant to ward off evil.

Whipping around, Cindy came face-to-face with the cloaked figure, way too close for comfort. Without thinking, she chucked the beads at its feet. It worked—the Lang Suyar stopped dead in its tracks, blocked by the beads. Its face, all creepy and wrinkled, twisted into a nasty snarl.

A wave of cold fear washed over Cindy at the sight of its freaky face, and she screamed her lungs out. Totally freaked out, she spun around and legged it, tearing through the dark, spooky paths of the cemetery. Her heart was pounding like crazy, fear fuelling her sprint towards the safety of the village.

As they headed back to town, Jax couldn't shake off her guilt about Esmerelda. Doc tried to make her feel better. "Jax, you did everything you could. Remember, you called the cops about Ti's boyfriend."

Jax was staring out the car window, lost in her thoughts, when she suddenly noticed a bunch of villagers gathered together. "Doc, stop the car. Something's going on there."

They parked and joined the crowd in the village. A teenage girl was in the middle, telling everyone a story. The villagers were all ears, looking scared and upset. Jax saw a policeman and went up to him.

"Do you speak English?" she asked.

"Yes," he answered, his gold tooth catching the light.

"What's she saying?" Jax wanted to know.

"The girl's saying she was chased by the Lang Suyar in the cemetery just now," he explained.

"Did she see who it was?" Jax asked, as Doc came up next to her.

"She says it was Esmerelda Kucing."

"That can't be right. We just found Esmerelda's body in the Belud River by the Hantu Pulp Mill. We already told the police," Jax said quickly.

The policeman nodded, remembering the call about Esmerelda and the arrest of Ti's boyfriend. He looked confused. "Then who killed Esmerelda?"

Jax quickly filled Doc in on what she'd just heard. They both knew this was serious and said at the same time, "Let's go!"

Jax walked over to the teenager, who was still talking. Despite Cindy's protests, Jax gently got her into the back of their car. "We need you to take us to where you saw the Lang Suyar," she said urgently.

The car headlights cut through the rolling mist like lasers. Driving through the cemetery gates felt like entering the set of a horror film.

They could go no further than the car park. Cindy pointed at the footpath. They had no choice but to continue on foot,

Doc opened the glove box, retrieved two pistols the police had given him, and handed one to Jax. "Can you handle this?"

"Do fish swim? But why now and not back at the mill?"

"It might've got you into trouble. Security guards are generally armed."

They got out of the car. As they walked towards the path leading through the decrepit cemetery, the creepiness intensified with every step. Mist snaked between the tombstones, some neglected, others toppled over, a few adorned with fresh flowers. Overhead, a full moon cast eerie shadows over grave markers, including statues of angels and crucifixes. The path was lined with gnarled trees, their branches reaching out like bony fingers. This wasn't the place for a casual evening stroll. Jax could tell Cindy was about to bolt, so she showed her the pistol to calm her down.

Hidden behind a crypt, the Lang Suyar watched them, its grotesque face twisted in anticipation, eyes burning yellow. It sniffed the air, sensing its prey was near.

They moved cautiously, the path leading them deeper into the heart of the graveyard, surrounded by the towering figures of ancient fig trees. Suddenly, a rustling noise startled Doc. Then, deep in the cemetery, the flap of an owl's wings rattled them. The distant howl of a dog pierced the night, it was hair-raising stuff. With his pistol aimed and a trembling finger on the trigger, Doc scanned the area. Nothing. Ahead, lined with big fig trees, the path led to the oldest part of the cemetery, dominated by a huge rain tree. Its towering presence allowed moonlight to filter through. Doc halted them just short of the rain tree, sensing something. Looking up, he spotted a large black dog perched on a thick lower branch, snarling menacingly. He aimed his pistol at it, alerting the others to the danger. "Back away, guys, this thing's bad news."

Jax gripped Cindy's arm, and they retreated. The dog pounced, landing on Doc and propelling him backwards. His head struck a tombstone hard, knocking him out cold. The dog stood over Doc, snarling and drooling. Overwhelmed, Cindy wrenched free from Jax and fled. The dog's attention shifted to Cindy. As it was about to chase her, Jax aimed and fired her gun. The recoil caused her to miss, and the bullet ricocheted off a tombstone. The dog, startled, unnaturally sprang up into a tree. Jax kept her gun trained on it, snarling down at her, as she knelt to check on Doc.

Growling, the big black dog leapt from the branch. Mid-air, it transformed into the grotesque, yellow-eyed Lang Suyar. It landed and charged at Jax, knocking the gun from her hand. Thinking quickly, Jax fumbled in her pocket for her laser pointer. As the creature, claws raised and mouth snarling, advanced, she shone the laser at its face. It backed off, trying to shield its eyes. Spotting the gun on the ground, Jax dived for it, propped herself up on one elbow and fired three quick shots. The creature, surprised, collapsed face down.

Jax got to her feet and approached it cautiously to confirm its death. Aiming her gun, she used her foot to roll it over. The creature was dead, but shockingly, it was Esmeralda.

Doc stirred. Jax went and assisted him up.

"You alright?"

Doc, feeling the back of his head, found blood. "Man, I think I cracked my head open. How long was I out?" he asked, sounding pretty out of it.

"Look, I shot the dog, but it was Esmeralda," Jax said, showing him where the body should be. But instead of Esmeralda, there was just a big, dead black dog. Jax didn't even try to explain what happened while Doc was out. She knew he probably wouldn't believe it. The eerie silence of the cemetery enveloped them as they stood there, the weight of the night's surreal events pressing down on them.

CHAPTER SIX

Back in Doc's hotel room, he was checking his emails. There was one from the lab in Kuala Lumpur where he'd sent the water samples. Jax was lost in thought, trying to piece together the night's weird events.

"I got the water test results," Doc announced. Jax got up and joined him at his laptop. Doc read out loud, "The water's got a seriously high level of Methyl Mercury. That stuff's super toxic—says, it causes birth defects and miscarriages in humans and animals." He looked up at Jax with a convinced look. "That's it. The village's water supply's messed up because of the mill's waste. Hantu probably knew and wanted Esmerelda's land to control the water source. He'd pipe clean water to the village at a huge price, making a fortune. All the while, he keeps using Methyl Mercury to keep his profits high—it's like environmental blackmail."

Jax was biting her knuckle, deep in thought. "I'm not sure that explains everything. Why wouldn't other villages downstream be affected too?"

"Because as the river gets wider, the contamination gets diluted," Doc explained.

Jax headed to her room, not really buying the whole contamination theory but totally sure that Esmerelda was the Lang Suyar.

The next morning, Doc and Jax met at the coffee shop for breakfast. Doc was all upbeat, but Jax looked like she hadn't slept a wink.

"What time's our flight?" Doc asked.

"Eleven," she replied, sounding a bit off.

"You okay?"

"Not really. I'm not sold on the contamination being the only cause. I know what I saw last night, and that was Esmerelda," Jax insisted.

"But then who did we find in the river?" Doc questioned.

"That's what kept me up half the night. I read in my Malay folklore book, the only way to kill a Lang Suyar is when it's in its witch form. I saw the dog transform into a seriously gross witch when it jumped from the tree. I shot it, and it turned into Esmerelda. Then, while I was helping you, it must've transformed back into the dog."

"That might fly for the TV show, Jax, but it's hard to believe," Doc responded sceptically.

"Why don't you believe me?" She shot back, getting heated.

"I think you're getting too caught up in the superstition, ignoring the facts. Maybe the unexplainable appeals to you more ... I just don't see it that way."

Jax was steaming. She hated that they couldn't see eye to eye on this. It was the same in their last cases too. But then, as she calmed down a bit, she realised their different views actually made them a solid team, perfect for the Next Files.

She cracked a smile at Doc. "Do we agree to disagree then?"

"Yes, we do. But somewhere in my mind," he said, reaching out for a handshake.

Jax raised an eyebrow, puzzled. "What's that supposed mean?"

"What?"

"Somewhere in my mind."

"You'll find it out soon enough," he said, all mysterious, just as his mobile rang with the ringtone 'The Terrible Tango,' abruptly ending their convo.

The gold-toothed policeman, accompanied by four officers and a forensics team of three, were led through the compound of the paper mill by the security guard Doc had confronted the previous night. Exiting through an end gate in the fence, they made their way down to the riverbank. Here, they expected to find the body of Esmerelda Kucing, as reported by Doc and Jax.

One of the officers, while searching, called out to the others. They quickly congregated to see his discovery. Instead of a body, they found only a green shroud.

The search continued for the rest of the day. They even brought in scuba divers to scour the river, but no trace of Esmerelda's body was found.

There was no sign that Esmerelda ever returned to her house at the source of the Kota Belud River. She had previously left her last will and testament with a lawyer in Kota. In the event of her disappearance, her property was to be bequeathed to the people of Sabah, indefinitely. Esmerelda, it seemed, had foreseen the danger to her life. In the end, her actions prevented Mr Hantu from getting his hands on her land, keeping the river's source safe for the community.

Back in Sydney, Jax and Doc figured they'd chill for a bit before getting into writing about their insane experience. Doc was to focus on the science stuff in his part, while Jax planned to tell her story like a true journalist. They both needed a break to wrap their heads around everything—it was a lot to take in.

Jax was convinced Esmerelda was the Lang Suyar, especially since there hadn't been any weird stuff happening since she disappeared. But Doc, always looking at things straight-up, thought maybe the attacks stopped because the village folks and the mill guys were on high alert now. Still, he couldn't get the image of Esmerelda's body by the river out of his mind.

While they were letting it all sink in, Doc got the chance to debut a new song with his band, The Time Benders, at the Friend in Hand. He shot Jax a text inviting her.

The message was a bit of a surprise for Jax – she hadn't expected to hear from Doc so soon. She thought he'd be in full-on chill mode. But the thought of catching his band again was tempting, so she decided to check it out.

Jax, always cool with doing her own thing, rocked up at the Friend in Hand looking like a million bucks.

She noticed right off that The Time Benders had drawn a bigger crowd this time. Weaving through the packed room to the bar, she grabbed a beer. That's when she spotted Tilly in the crowd.

Strolling over, Jax teased, "Never pegged you for the rock concert type, Till."

"You might be surprised, girl. I'm the one who paid for all Doc's guitar lessons, you know."

"Oh, so you're here to see if your investment paid off?"

"Not exactly. I'm here for you. Doc mentioned you'd be coming. Follow me."

Tilly led Jax to a quieter spot. "I've been in touch with Digger."

Jax was stunned. "What! How did he...?"

"I reached out. Spent enough time around journalists to pick up a few tricks... your boss helped."

"Des?"

"That's right. Found him in Sydney. He should be here any minute."

Jax felt like her world was tilting. "What, Digger... here? But I..."

"Easy, girl. He's your brother, step or not. You grew up together. Time to let bygones be bygones. Welcome him back. I think he'd like that."

Jax gulped down her beer, maybe seeking a bit of liquid courage.

"Come on, Till, let's grab a drink." She hooked Tilly's arm and headed back to the bar, a mix of nerves and excitement bubbling inside her.

They had barely gotten their drinks when the house lights went down and the band kicked in. The stage lit up with Doc at the mic, his white Fender Stratocaster hanging coolly over his shoulder. Jax didn't recognise the tune at first, but as Doc began to sing, she realised it was a bluesy rendition of Stevie Wonder's 'Superstition'. The way he looked out over the crowd, she just knew he was singing it for her.

A minute into the song, Jax caught herself dancing. The music had that kind of pull. Then, as the band hit the second chorus – 'When you believe in things that you don't understand ... then you suffer...' – she felt a tap on her shoulder. Expecting Tilly, she turned around, only to come face-to-face with her stepbrother, Digger. For a second, she just froze. Then, as tears welled up in her eyes, she wrapped him in a tight hug.

They were both in tears, and when Tilly joined the hug, all three of them were crying. It was like a family reunion right there in the middle of the concert. Once they'd gotten over the initial shock of seeing each other after seven long years, they took a moment to really look at each other, the band's music playing in the background.

Jax noticed the hardship in Digger's eyes. Only six months older than her, he looked years beyond that now. Standing as tall as Doc at 6' 2", he seemed pretty tall for a First Nations guy, especially since he'd been shorter than her back when they were last together in Manila. He had this sturdy build and a tough, no-nonsense look in his eyes, but Jax could sense a hint of uncertainty there too.

Digger was taking in his sister, seeing how she'd changed from the girl he remembered to the woman before him now. She had the beauty and figure of their mother and the eyes of her father, but what really stood out was her intelligence, shining through just like their mum's.

Several songs later, Doc's voice brought them back from their thoughts.

"I know my friend Jax is here tonight ... This next song is about some wild stuff we've been through. It's for you, Jax. It's called 'Somewhere in my Mind'."

Jax instantly flashed back to their conversation at the hotel in Kota—when Doc had said those words, and she'd asked what he meant. He'd told her she'd find out one day. Well, today was that day.

The song started with an enigmatic Middle Eastern vibe, and then Doc's voice filled the room.

I'm a voice in the dark
And I call out to you
It's such a lonely sound

I'm a king in the rain
Lost down and blue
A king without a crown

Somewhere in my mind it's raining
Washing out all that's true
Yes, somewhere in my mind it's raining
Somewhere in my mind there's you

Doc played a guitar solo.

Time and again
I hear fate calling me
Like lions in the den
I need to pick up the pieces and then
start all over again
Start again…

I walk in deep dark dreams
Through fields of the lost
There's nothing left to find

There's voices inside
there's no place to hide
they leave me flying blind

Somewhere in my mind it's raining
Washing out all that's true
Yes, somewhere in my mind it's raining
Somewhere in my mind there's you

Doc launched into another guitar solo.

Somewhere in my mind it's raining
Washing out all that's true
Yes, somewhere in my mind it's raining
Somewhere in my mind there's you

Somewhere in my mind it's raining
Washing out all that's true
Yes, somewhere in my mind it's raining
Somewhere in my mind there's you

Somewhere in my mind it's raining
Washing out all that's true
Yes, somewhere in my mind it's raining
Somewhere in my mind there's you

Somewhere in my mind it's raining
Washing out all that's true
Yes, somewhere in my mind it's raining
Somewhere in my mind there's you

CHAPTER SEVEN

Post-gig, Jax, Doc, Digger, and Tilly grabbed a bite at a nearby restaurant, diving into a long overdue catch-up. Jax started off, recounting her adventures since their last meeting. As she talked about landing the job at NewsLine and taking over the Next Files, it all felt surreal, like she was narrating a bizarre fairy tale. She left out the bit about their father's diary, thinking it was something to share with Digger later, in private.

Then it was Digger's turn to share his story. He had this rough, smoker-like voice, but he didn't actually smoke. He told them about his search for his roots up in far north Queensland. It hadn't worked out, so he ended up with a job at an opal mine near the town of Eromanga, in Western Queensland.

"When I say town," he rasped, "Eromanga's so far-flung, there's a sign saying 'Eromanga, furthest town from the sea'. We're talking about 1,440 kilometres from here, to give you an idea of just how remote it is. The place has like twenty houses and a tin shed they call The Royal Hotel. You'd see blokes landing their planes right in front of the pub for a beer run. I was in a mining camp about sixty clicks north of there. Just fifteen guys, a couple of bulldozers, all open cut, tough as. Then things went south when the cook lost it and attacked someone with a meat cleaver. That was my cue to get out. Found myself in Brisbane when I saw Jax's name on a TV show. Figured it was time to hit the big city, find my sister. Old Tilly's been writing to me, keeping me in the loop. She's a legend."

"Hey, watch who you're calling old," Tilly joked with a hearty laugh.

Doc chimed in, "So what's next for you, man?"

"Well, Tilly's hooked me up with a place to crash at hers while I figure things out," Digger said, running his fingers through his long black hair.

"And what kind of work are you looking for?" Jax asked.

Digger grinned at Doc. "Honestly? I can do a bit of everything. Heck, I'd join a band like yours if I could make a buck."

"What do you play?" Doc inquired, interested.

"I'm pretty decent with a harmonica, can play a mean didgeridoo, and I can sing," Digger replied, flashing a bright smile.

"I might need some help with research at the Next Files, and a part-time gig with The Time Benders could keep you busy," Jax suggested.

Tilly's voice turned serious. "You staying clear of booze and drugs?"

"Clean as a whistle," Digger assured.

Plans were set. Jax would talk to Des Carter about it the next day.

Later that night, Jax sat in her office chair at home, lost in thought. The reunion with Digger had stirred up a lot. She knew he had a deeper spiritual connection than her, something they hadn't delved into over dinner. She recalled his psychic bond with their mother and how he knew when she passed away. It had hit him hard, sending him on a quest for his Ancestor Spirits. Jax wondered if he had found what he was looking for. She mused on the concept of 'Dreamtime' or 'Tjukurrpa', better called 'The Dreaming', pondering its relevance to their shared Yalanji heritage.

An alert popped up on her computer, drawing her attention to a new email. It was from Doc, containing his account of the Lang Suyar story. As she had expected, his version was all science, no supernatural. It was a stark, pragmatic take on the events. Jax planned to merge it with her own summary for a comprehensive report to Janet, her producer.

Opening the document where she'd been drafting her editorial, Jax began to write the final summary:

"Doc Lee suggests that two of the four miscarriages in Kampong Lobong-Lobong village were due to either intentional termination or Methyl Mercury contamination in the drinking water. The other two cases might be linked to witchcraft. From my perspective, the vanishing act of Esmerelda Kucing indicates that, as the villagers suspected, she was the Lang Suyar. If that's true, then I believe I shot and killed Esmerelda while she was in a lycanthropic state, taking the form of a dog. However, since we only found the dog's body and no human remains, we can't confirm this theory. Therefore, the case remains unresolved, or 'non-lequet'.

"Doc's report states the dog's body was later autopsied and blood samples taken. DNA testing revealed pseudogenes present, these are genes no longer functional in most humans but, though rare, many of them are functional in some people.

"Let's just say that lycanthropy could possibly convert DNA to human/werewolf hybrid DNA, and then the physiological changes would need to be magical.

"In conclusion, both Doc and I recommend shutting down the Hantu Paper Mill until it meets the World Health Organisation's standards. We also suggest that the mill provide compensation and medical care to the affected villagers and supply them with clean water, free of charge."

The next morning, Jax had a meeting with her boss, Des Carter. Despite craving some downtime, she reminded herself of the opportunity at NewsLine as she entered Carter's office.

Carter gestured for her to sit down as he wrapped up a phone call. Once off the phone, he looked at Jax across his desk. "You know, Jax, you really are a chip off the old block. Your Lang Suyar story is going to be a hit. The audience will love it. Janet's already buzzing about it."

Jax felt a surge of pride. "Thank you, sir."

"So, what's next on the agenda for the Next Files?" Carter asked.

Jax shifted in her seat, still unsure. "I'm not quite certain yet."

"Did you manage to meet up with Digger?" he inquired.

"Yes, and thank you for your help with that," Jax replied.

"It was nothing. So, he's going to join your team? You might need a bigger office for you both," Carter hinted with a smile.

This news made Jax even happier. "That would be great."

"Janet will show you to your new office soon. We've started digitizing the Next Files so you won't be buried in boxes," Carter informed her.

Jax let out a relieved sigh. "That's great. A lot of those files are outdated."

"But it's always good to have them on record," Carter added.

Jax nodded. "I'm planning to focus on the more recent cases. Digger will help with that. Uh, I'll need a day or two before diving back in ... I've got some important things to discuss with Digger."

"Of course. Take your time. Family's important. How's he doing?" Carter asked.

"He's changed, but I can still see the boy he used to be," Jax replied.

"You'll always see that. I'm the same with my siblings," Carter empathised, standing up. "Sort things out with Digger, then let me know what your next adventure will be."

As Jax was leaving, Janet came in and hugged her excitedly. "The Lang Suyar story is fantastic! A mix of ecology, science and myth—it's brilliant! Tell me, did you really shoot that thing?"

Jax confirmed, "Yes," feeling a mixture of pride and disbelief.

Janet, arm around Jax, guided her out of Carter's office, excited to show her the new workspace. They arrived at an office with 'The Next Files, Executive Producer, Jax de Loite' frosted on the glass doors. Inside, the office was impressive—a big window with a stunning view, spacious, with two desks. Janet then introduced Jax to Donna, her new secretary. Jax, overwhelmed with excitement, barely found words to express her gratitude.

Later, Jax met with Digger at a Starbucks in The Rocks. She had prepared a surprise for him—a private ascent to the top of the Sydney Harbour Bridge. The climb leader granted them solitude at the zenith for twenty minutes. Under a cloudless sky, they just sat and chilled, the city sprawling beneath them. Time zipped by super fast.

Walking off the bridge, Digger was totally blown away. "That was extraordinary, I can't thank you enough."

Jax grabbed the moment to talk about something weird. "When I was in Queensland recently, I was visited by a spirit only I could see. I thought he was a Kadaitcha man. But I learned in Alice Springs he's my spirit guide, Jibbi Jib."

Digger stopped cold, gripping Jax's shoulders. "Jibbi Jib came to me too."

Jax was shocked. "What do you think he wants?"

"I think he has information about our father but is waiting to share it with both of us."

Jax mulled that over. "Can we contact him again?"

"Yes, we need to hold a Pituri Ceremony to reach the Dreaming. Time is different for our people. Jibbi Jib might be a relative from the past. I'm here to guide you there."

"Have you been to the Dreaming?"

"Yes, in Boulia, Western Queensland, the land of the Pituri."

"Boulia? That's where I covered the Min Min light story."

"You were drawn there, Jax. It wasn't just coincidence."

"Do we need to go back there?"

"No, we can get Pituri here in Sydney. We'll hold our Ceremony here."

Jax's mind raced with the idea of starting this spiritual adventure with Digger, stepping into a world they didn't fully get but felt deeply connected to.

"Have you ever sensed anything about Dad?" Jax asked, a hint of curiosity in her voice.

Digger paused, his gaze distant. "Yeah, like maybe he wants us to track him. But I don't have any clues about his disappearance."

Jax reached into her bag and pulled out a rugged, dark green book. She handed it to Digger. "Here."

He looked at the book, a bit puzzled. "What's this? You know I'm still not big on reading…"

"Dad's diary," Jax explained, "It covers everything up until he vanished. A search party found it in the jungle."

Digger's eyes widened in astonishment, his hands quivering as he held the diary. It seemed as if he were grasping a fragment of history, a lost artefact. The diary, laden with significance, felt like a tangible connection to the father he presumed lost forever.

BLOOD OF THE AZTECS

CHAPTER ONE

"I was only seven when they came. That was ten years ago," the young man murmured, his head lowered, his long brown hair shrouding his face. The arrival of the invaders had upended his world. Chained at his wrists and ankles, he was connected in a long line with other captive boys and girls his age. They were seated on the wharf, their backs to the aqua waters of Acapulco Bay, their despair overshadowing its natural beauty.

The girl next to him muttered, "Some say they will drown us."

"No, if that were their intention, they would've done it by now. We must stay strong. We have an advantage..."

"How can you say that while we're in chains?"

"They don't understand our language."

Indeed, the Aztec language, Nahuatl, was foreign to the Spanish marines guarding them. Overhearing the conversation, a bulky, armoured marine turned sharply and lashed out with his cane, striking the young man across the back.

"Silencio!" the marine barked in Spanish, a stern command for silence.

The young man winced, biting his lip to suppress his pain.

As the guard patrolled the line of twenty prisoners, tapping the cane menacingly into his palm, the boy asked his fellow prisoner, "What's your name?"

"I am Neza, and you?"

"Neza, meaning rain; a divine gift. They call me Ocelot, for the small jaguar, but my true name is Meshika."

"Meshika, a name for leaders, meant for royalty," Neza said, astounded.

"Yes, I am the grandson of the late King Moctezuma."

Neza, of ordinary lineage, was surprised to find herself chained next to a descendant of the Aztec throne.

"I want to kill him," Neza whispered fiercely, "he beat my brother to death yesterday."

"Don't worry, Neza. Our time will come; we must be shrewd and patient."

"Is this the end of our culture, Ocelot?"

"No, not as long as I carry it."

"Where do you carry it?"

"In my blood, Neza. It's in my blood."

Just then, a shadow fell over them. They looked up to see the sails of a massive Spanish galleon docking at the wharf. Ocelot read the name inscribed on the ship's bow and muttered in Spanish, "Nuestra Señora de la Concepción."

"What does that mean?" Neza whispered.

"It is the name of this ship that will take us to a new world."

Jax and Digger emerged from an old house in La Perouse. Shielding her eyes from the intense noon sun, Jax remarked, "I've got brain fog after that. You too?"

"It'll clear. The Pituri clouds the mind while opening it."

"Let's sit on the rock across the road and gaze at the water."

They crossed the park, clambered over a low picket fence, and perched on a rocky outcrop overlooking the shimmering blue waters of the bay below.

"That's Congwong Bay, locals nickname it Little Congo."

"How do you know about it and the elders back in the house?"

"I spent a few weeks in Sydney after arriving from Manila. I wanted to visit the site where the colonists landed. It's over there, across Botany Bay at Kurnell. There's a memorial. Interestingly, the British named it Kurnell, a corruption of the Aboriginal word 'Cunnel', meaning family. Ironic, huh?"

Jax pondered, admiring Digger's quest to understand his heritage and culture, a journey she felt compelled to embark on herself.

"Have you left the Ceremony with more questions than answers?" she asked, as a southerly breeze swept her hair back like a banner.

"Yes, but it has deepened our connection to the Dreaming, and we've learned something new."

"That maybe dad is alive, and…" Jax trailed off.

"That we already possess the means to find him."

"That's a bit cryptic for me," Jax admitted.

"I think it's in the diary, maybe coded. Dad loved puzzles."

"True. He was obsessed with deciphering codes."

"Mum was the same. Goes with being an archaeologist, right?"

Jax rose, inhaling deeply the ocean air. A kookaburra perched on the fence laughed, which Jax interpreted as Jibbi Jib keeping an eye on them.

"Let's head to the office. Time to get back to work."

"Has the fog lifted?"

"Yes, the magic of this special place cleared it."

It was time for Jax to pitch the next episode to Des Carter. She felt a surge of confidence after her morning with Digger in La Perouse and their visit to the Dreaming. Yet, once she was sitting across from Carter, his expectant gaze made a bit of insecurity creep in.

Opening her pitch, she said, "When we were kids, Dad used to tell us about a boy called Ocelot, the grandson of Moctezuma, the king of the Aztec empire that was conquered by Cortez. It was like a metaphor for how, two hundred and fifty years later, the Aboriginals in this country were conquered by the British."

"If your story is about that, Jax, we can't get involved in cultural issues…"

"No, it's not that, I'm just setting the scene … So, this Ocelot story, which means 'small jaguar', originally came from a 1997 archaeological expedition by Dad and Mum in Mindanao."

"Before you or Digger were born."

"Yeah, Digger is ten months older than me. The expedition aimed to find where the first mass in the Philippines was held. A

Venetian scholar, Antonio Pigafetta, who was on Magellan's ship Trinidad, kept a detailed journal."

"This was what, 1521, right?"

"Yes. Pigafetta wrote about the mass and the importance of bringing Christianity to the new land but didn't specify the exact location, only that it was the first landfall."

"Okay, go on," Carter said, now intrigued.

"Well, the first landfall was actually the island of Guam, but they found it unfriendly, so they moved on. About a month later, they landed on the island of Homonhon in the south of Mindanao. Finding no fresh water there, and after sighting fishing boats, they moved on again and eventually landed at Limasawa Island. That's where they presumably held the first mass. With all the conjecture, Mum and Dad got funding from the Philippine government to go to Limasawa to search for evidence of the mass."

"I think I remember Henry telling me about this."

"He probably did. They found nothing, but when a local fisherman told them about a piece of a Spanish galleon near Surigao on the mainland of Mindanao, they paid him to take them to see it."

"Fascinating. Where is this going, Jax?"

She pressed on, trying to keep his interest, "Dad was half Filipino, half Mexican—and his Mexican side wasn't Spanish, it was Aztec."

"I didn't know that. So, you're half Aztec, half Aboriginal?"

"Yes, but not Digger, he's full-blood Aboriginal."

"Got it, keep going," Carter said, rotating a pen masterfully between his fingers.

"Dad always believed that the first ships to arrive in the Philippines after Magellan's expedition carried Aztec slaves. Shortly after Cortez conquered the Aztecs, Magellan discovered the Philippines in 1521. Once Mexico was colonised, by 1530 the Spanish used Acapulco as a port. It was a far shorter route to the Philippines than going from Spain around South America. They decided to revisit Cebu, where Magellan had been killed. Dad wanted to prove his theory that Aztec slaves on those early expeditions had escaped into the jungles of Mindanao and continued the Aztec customs."

"Yes, I know his theory. It's what claimed the lives of both your parents. Where's this going, Jax?"

"They found something. It's mentioned in his diary..."

"I told you to leave that until another time," he protested.

"I didn't find it, Digger did ... The fisherman showed them a small section of old ship's wood with 'Nuestra Señora...'"

"So?"

"They knew it had to be part of the name of a Spanish galleon, and they were right. It was the Nuestra Señora de la Concepción, one of three ships sent from Acapulco on the first expedition to the Philippines since Magellan had been killed there."

"Okay, and then?"

"They went to Mexico later that year to check maritime records. The ship had foundered on a reef, and the crew was saved aboard the other two ships. But a landing party of slaves had been sent into the jungle for provisions, and they never made it back. The ship's manifest confirmed that the Nuestra Señora de la Concepción was carrying twenty Aztec slaves, and that none of them returned from the expedition. One of those slaves was Ocelot, believed to be the grandson of Moctezuma."

"I see, so that's the origin of your father's bedtime story?"

"Yes, and we believe he found a tribe of Aztecs that still exists in the jungles of Mindanao, relatives of those twenty slaves."

"No, Jax, it's too dangerous."

"Tell me a better story for The Next Files?"

"No, but it's a story for later, once you're more seasoned."

"But if what if he's alive, we need to find him," she protested.

"That's not our job. We make television programming. Besides, it's all speculation."

"No, it isn't. We've been told he lived."

"By whom?"

"Digger took me to a Pituri Ceremony this morning. I visited the Dreaming. My spirit guide told me Dad was still in the jungle and that the diary holds the key to his location."

Carter stared at Jax, unsure how to take what she'd just told him.

"A Pituri Ceremony? The Dreaming?"

"It's a cultural thing. You need to believe me, Des. Dad's a friend of yours. It was on your watch that we lost him."

"I know, I know… but…"

CHAPTER TWO

The success of The Next Files and Des Carter's benevolence had given Jax the chance to search for her father. Now, the task was to get Doc on board. With Digger staying with Doc and Tilly, Jax knew they'd been softening him up. Her mission that morning was to clinch the deal so they could start organizing the expedition.

She called Digger to arrange a meeting at Tilly's place to persuade Doc.

As the coffee brewed and Doc relaxed in the sunroom, Digger greeted Jax at the door. Since the Pituri Ceremony, their brother-sister relationship had deepened, tapping into a spiritual kinship. They grabbed coffees and joined Doc, who set aside his newspaper to accept a mug from Jax.

"Well, don't you look radiant today," Doc complimented Jax. "Tilly mentioned you had a meeting with the boss. How did it go? Do we have our next file?"

Jax, with a smug smile, sipped her coffee, then placed a folder on the table. "As a matter of fact, we do." She slid the folder across to Doc.

He read the one-page synopsis inside, then looked up, puzzled. "Ocelot? A slave on a Spanish galleon? I don't quite follow."

Jax, having already pitched the idea to Carter, refined her delivery for Doc. She smoothly explained the connection of the Aztecs in the Philippines to her family. Meanwhile, Digger refilled their coffee mugs as Jax waited for Doc's reaction.

"You're saying he could be alive?"

"Yes."

"And you and Digger found this out from your spirit guide? Was it Jibbi Jib from Boulia and Alice Springs?"

"That's right."

Doc rubbed his chin, pondering. "So, this is a setup."

"What do you mean?"

"Tilly and Digger have been prepping me for your pitch, right?"

As Digger handed out the refilled mugs, he admitted, "We were just priming you, so Jax's explanation wouldn't seem too far-fetched."

"Since meeting your sister, Digger, everything's been far-fetched," Doc remarked smugly.

Digger chuckled. "Yeah, I guess so."

"Okay, okay, I get it. I'm outnumbered. What's the plan? Do you have a location?"

Jax and Digger exchanged glances. "Jibbi Jib said we already have the location."

"That's a bit cryptic."

"It's in the diary," Digger interjected.

Jax leaned in. "Dad loved codes, like decoding hieroglyphs and ancient texts. We think there's something in the last pages of the diary that pinpoints his location."

Digger brought out the diary. "I've read the last chapter repeatedly but can't find anything, except a reference to Awtadi. Googled it, found nothing."

"How's it used?" asked Jax.

Digger flipped to the page. "Here..."

Doc took the book, reading aloud, "We search for the source of the Surigao River, a region rich in cultural history. The indigenous people are highly superstitious about Awtadi."

"You know the guy, what do you think he's trying to hide, and why?" Doc asked.

Jax and Digger exchanged that knowing look again. Jax spoke up, "I reckon he'd be hiding his actual location."

Doc nodded, having suspected as much. "Yes, but why?"

"Because if he was right and there's still an Aztec culture hidden in the jungles, he wouldn't want to risk exposing them," Digger explained.

"That makes sense," Doc conceded. "Like that tribe in the Amazon rainforest discovered a few years back, kept secret to protect them. Where did Cindy, your mother, disappear?"

"Near the source of the Surigao River," Digger revealed.

"Dad's old mate and guide, Ito Santos, from Davao City, vanished with Dad. He'd know the GPS location of where Mum disappeared."

"Do you think they vanished at the same place?" Doc inquired.

"Maybe," Digger speculated. "I reckon Awtadi might be the name of a place."

Jax, lost in thought, mused, "Ito's family night know."

Digger's eyes lit up. "That's where we should start looking."

"Davao?" Jax questioned.

"Yeah, let's track down the Santos family. Ito had a wife and kids, if I remember right. Maybe the GPS location is among Ito's belongings."

Jax interjected, "Wait, doesn't Tilly know Ito?"

Digger grinned, "I reckon Tilly knows more than we think."

Jax brought up another point. "There's also the apartment."

"What apartment?" Doc queried.

"Our old place in Manila," Jax said. "Loads of Dad's records are there."

"Still there, unoccupied?" Digger probed.

"Yes, it's ours. When I left to finish school here, Tilly moved out shortly after, leaving it vacant."

Digger leaned back, arms crossed. "Alright, we start with the apartment, then head to Davao."

"In the meantime, let's dig into what Awtadi means," suggested Doc. "Could save us a lot of legwork if we figure that out first."

Jax was deep into her work when Tilly popped into her office. "Where's Digger at, hon?"

Peering up from her computer, Jax answered, "He's hashing things out with Doc. We're set to fly to Manila tomorrow."

Tilly frowned. "I heard about that ... Look, I'm all for finding the truth about your dad, but the thought of losing you both scares me."

Jax stood up and hugged her. "Hey, don't sweat it, Till. We know what we're doing."

"That's just what your dad would say."

"We're crashing at our old Manila pad. Need to dig through dad's stuff for any leads."

"Leads to what?"

"Where he might be. Hey, Till, take a seat..." They sat down. "You knew Ito Santos, right?"

"Sure did. Introduced him to your dad. I've felt awful about it since ... I've been helping out his wife in Davao."

"We're hitting up the Santos family after Makati. Might find something at their place, like where mum went missing, GPS-wise."

"If it's there, it's tucked away good."

"Why's that?"

"Rafe Maddox."

"I don't think I've ever heard that name, who is he?"

"Your dad kept all that kind of stuff from you ... Des Carter knows who he is ... real badass. Your dad was always hiding stuff from him. Des can tell you more, go ask him."

Jax didn't muck about, she made a beeline for Des Carter's office.

Des shouted from inside, "Come in..."

Jax entered. "Got a sec, boss?"

"Sure. Actually wanted to chat with you too. But unload first."

"What's the deal with Rafe Maddox?"

Des leaned back. "He's why I wanted to talk. Rafe Maddox, trouble with a capital T. Deals in stolen relics, used to work for the CIA. He's all over Southeast Asia, looking for a big score. We tried to nab him at Eco Mag. If your dad found something big, and you find it, Maddox will be all over it."

"So he's on dad's trail too?"

"You can bet your life on it."

"Got anything on him?"

"I'll shoot you an email with the deets."

"Sweet." Jax was heading out when Des called to her.

"Jax, just a heads-up, Maddox isn't someone you want to mess with. Be very careful."

Stepping into The Colonnade Residences on Legazpi Street, Makati, felt like traveling back in time for Jax and Digger. They took the lift to the top floor penthouse. Inside, the air was stale, exactly what you'd expect from a place shut up for seven years. They didn't waste time getting nostalgic; instead, they jumped straight into making the place liveable.

By mid-afternoon, after sprucing up the condo, they uncovered the big old Chesterfield in the living room and collapsed into its comfortable embrace. The aircon had kicked in by then, offering a cool escape from the muggy heat outside.

"Lucky we all caught some z's on the flight, or we wouldn't have managed all this," Jax sighed, relaxing into the sofa.

"Your first time in Makati, Doc?" asked Digger.

"Yeah, feels a lot like KL. We were there earlier this year," Doc replied.

"The Lang Suyar," Digger joked, pulling a spooky face.

"I could really go for a cold beer," Jax mused.

Digger was quick to respond, "I'll grab us a slab. Why don't you start digging through Dad's office?"

Doc stood up too. "Need any help, Jax?"

"No, you guys go. I've got this."

Once Digger and Doc had gone, Jax took a deep breath, steeling herself for what lay ahead. She walked down the hallway, which felt more like a gateway into a world of exploration. The walls, adorned with an array of weapons and ceremonial masks from Asia and Central America, spoke volumes of her father's adventurous spirit.

Memories started to flood in, each artefact bringing a different story to mind. Overwhelmed, tears began to blur her vision. She paused, sinking into a chair just outside her father's office. In that quiet moment, she allowed herself to feel the full weight of her emotions.

After a few minutes, she composed herself and stood up. Beside the office door was the familiar large portrait of her dad, humorously labelled 'Henry Indiana de Loite'. A wave of nostalgia washed over her as she remembered her mother presenting it as a birthday gift when she was a toddler. A small smile crept onto her face as she gazed at the portrait.

Smiling at the memory, Jax reached for the doorknob, turned it, and with a click, stepped into a room untouched since her father left for his last expedition.

CHAPTER
THREE

Jax sifted through the piles of papers and research in her dad's office. There was an overwhelming amount on the birdman cult, almost to the point of obsession. She stumbled upon articles from his peers, openly mocking his theory, particularly after he claimed to have seen his wife, Cindy, taken by a birdman. She felt a pang of sympathy; her dad must have felt so isolated without anyone backing his hypothesis.

But then, among the papers, Jax found a letter from Des Carter. It was a lifeline of support, offering financial backing for an expedition to find the birdman cult for Eco Magazine. The date on the letter aligned with her dad's final expedition. No wonder Carter harboured a sense of guilt.

Just then, she heard Digger and Doc return. Digger's voice echoed through the halls, inviting her to join them for a beer. As she prepared to leave the office, her eyes caught sight of a notepad by the phone. Four words were scribbled on it, all unfamiliar, except one – 'Nicyd'. It sparked a childhood memory; 'Nicyd' was an anagram she used for fun, a playful rearrangement of her mother's name, Cindy. The realisation hit her like a bolt of lightning. The mysterious word 'Awtadi' from the diary—could it also be an anagram?

Excited by this revelation, she hurried into the living room to share her discovery with Digger and Doc. Perhaps this was the key they needed to unlock the location her father had so cryptically hinted at.

She was greeted with a cold beer, which was most welcome.

"Cheers," Digger said, perched on the arm of the Chesterfield.

Doc, standing by the window, raised his bottle, "Yes, best of luck."

"Did you find anything?" Digger asked Jax.

"A whole pile of memories. We pretty much kept out of the office, so it was a trip, especially with it being as he left it."

"That's spooky," Digger said.

"But … I found something. Remember we used to mess with anagrams?"

"Yeah, it was one of dad's favourite games."

"Well, I think 'Awtadi' isn't a place; it's the anagram of one."

Doc ambled over, sat down on the lounge, and entered 'Awtadi' into AI on his phone. He called out the results, "Tawaid, Diwata, Watadi…"

Jax was entering each word into AI on her phone, asking if it was a place name in Mindanao. "Stop," she told Doc, "Got it. The Diwata Mountains are known for their rich biodiversity, with various endemic species of flora and fauna. They are also the source of several rivers, including the Surigao River, which flows through the city of Surigao and empties into the Surigao Strait."

Digger, also on his phone, inputted the word into AI and read out his results, "Get this … 'the Diwata Mountains have a rich cultural history, with the indigenous people of the region considering the mountain range sacred and the home of the Diwata, or deities, in their traditional beliefs.' And this … 'the word "Diwata" is derived from the ancient Sanskrit word "Devata," which means "deity" or "divine being." It is a term used in Philippine mythology to refer to a type of nature spirit or deity that is often associated with natural features such as forests, mountains, rivers, and the sea. Diwatas are believed to possess supernatural powers and are often depicted as benevolent guardians of nature, although some stories also portray them as mischievous or vengeful.'"

"I wonder if the people in that region think of the Diwatas as birdmen?" Jax proposed.

"You might be right," Doc said, again reading from his phone. "Says here, 'the Manok is a birdwoman or man of local folklore in Mindanao, that inhabit the forest.' Knowing how superstitious people in the region are, you'd expect they'd keep clear of a place thought to be inhabited by supernatural creatures."

"You get extreme superstition in highly religious societies," Jax added.

"Okay, we have a place; the Diwata Mountains, we have mention of the source of the Surigao River in the diary," Doc said.

"That's one big hunk of country, all of it seriously dense rainforest," Digger claimed.

Jax was nodding in agreement with them. "What we need is the GPS location of where mum vanished."

"Surely your father would have written that down somewhere," Doc expounded.

"If it wasn't for two facts, one, the rejection of his hypothesis by academia and two, probably the more critical; he wouldn't risk having the location exposed to Rafe Maddox."

"Who's that?" both Doc and Digger asked at the same time.

Jax got her briefcase and took out a document. "Tilly and Des Carter knew about this guy," she handed the document to Doc, who read it out.

"An ex-CIA 42-year-old American, deals in stolen relics notably from south east Asia. Has been busted a bunch of times, wanted in a number of countries including the USA and Australia. Presumed to be a resident of the Philippines and dangerous." He handed it to Digger. "Nice, so this guy was your dad's nemesis? So we're up against an uninhabited impenetrable tropical jungle, a birdman cult, and an ex-CIA black marketeer killer ... not the best of odds."

In a restless sweat, Jax tossed and turned in bed. She rolled onto her back, her eyes snapping open as the ceiling fan above her slowed to a surreal, almost hypnotic spin, emitting an eerie 'swishing' noise. Time itself seemed distorted, stretched thin. Sitting up, she reached to brush her hair away from her face, but her hand moved with a stuttering, jerky motion, as if she were seeing a series of still images rather than one fluid movement. It lingered in her vision, creating a bizarre illusion of multiple hands trailing behind.

Staring into the room's enveloping darkness, a creeping sense of unease washed over her. She sensed a presence, something or someone lurking just beyond her sight. From the depths of the pitch-black room, a figure emerged—a snake-headed birdman, its claws menacingly poised as if ready to strike. Jax's heart raced; her breath caught in her throat. But before the creature could reach her, it shifted, transforming before her eyes into the familiar face of her father. As she watched, bewildered and terrified, it morphed again, this time taking on the form of her mother. Her mother, a ghostly image, stood at the bed's end, arms outstretched, inviting Jax towards her with an ethereal, silent beckoning.

Then, as suddenly as the visions appeared, the room was lit by a harsh, blinding flash of light. Jax found herself standing in a different place, gazing down at a casket set deep in an open grave. The coffin lid began to slide open slowly, creaking with the weight of dread and finality. Inside, to her horror, was herself, motionless and lifeless.

Jax woke up with a start, her heart racing, pounding fiercely in her chest. She gasped for air, trying to orient herself in the still-dark room. Her mind was a whirlwind of confusion and fear, the remnants of the dream lingering like a haunting echo. She wiped the cold sweat from her brow, her breathing gradually slowing as the terror of the nightmare began to recede. But the images—the snake-headed birdman, her father, her mother, and the coffin—clung to the edges of her consciousness, a lingering reminder of the dream's unsettling vividness.

Digger ambled into the lounge room yawning and was surprised to find Jax curled up on the lounge, asleep. He sat on the arm of the lounge and nudged her. "Morning, why did you sleep here?"

Jax woke up and sat up, rubbing the sleep from her eyes. "Nightmares. Horrible nightmare. A frightening birdman was standing at the end of the bed, just staring at me. At first, I thought it was real, then it morphed into Dad, then Mum."

Digger patted her on the knee. "It's been massive for you, sis. Being back in the old apartment, it's no wonder you're having nightmares."

Doc wandered out in blue and white striped pyjamas, stopped, and stretched. "Hey, what's going on?"

"Well, if it isn't B1, or is it B2?" Jax teased, referring to the '90s TV show Bananas in Pyjamas.

"Sis had nightmares, saw a birdman. Ended up sleeping out here," Digger explained.

Doc yawned. "Is there any coffee?"

"No, but there's a Starbucks opposite," Jax replied.

At 8 am, the tropical humidity was already intense. Doc stepped out of the air-conditioned comfort of the condo lobby, only for his sunglasses to instantly fog up. Temporarily blinded, he stumbled on the front stairs, eliciting chuckles from Jax and Digger.

A short while later, after a brisk walk under the increasingly scorching sun, they found refuge under an umbrella in the alfresco section of a nearby Starbucks. They settled in for breakfast, the sunny morning promising an even hotter day ahead.

"My armpits are leaking," Doc groaned, wiping his forehead with the back of his hand.

Digger, ever the realist, chimed in, "Better get used to it, pal. It's going to be a whole lot worse in the jungle."

Jax, meanwhile, was absorbed in her phone, tapping away as she secured their travel plans. She had just finished booking seats on a flight to Davao. Tilly had provided her with crucial details—the address of the Santos family in Davao and the name of the curator of the Davao Museum, who had deep knowledge of her father's last expedition.

The three of them sipped their drinks, the bustle of the city surrounding them. For Jax, each step closer to Davao felt like a step closer to unravelling the mysteries that had long hovered over her family's history.

A few hours later, they were soaring through the skies towards Davao City.

After landing, they quickly checked into a nearby hotel. Once settled, they reconvened in the lobby and hailed a cab to the Davao Museum. The drive to Museo Dabaweyno was brief. Jax, having anticipated their needs, had already arranged a meeting with the museum's curator, Dr Christina Jimenez, via phone.

They were guided through the small museum to the back of the two-storey building, into the curator's office. Dr Christina Jimenez, a bespectacled woman in her early forties, greeted them with a warm and welcoming manner. She had the poise and appearance reminiscent of an academic or a librarian, which added to her charm.

Inviting them to sit in a comfortable lounge area of her office, she prepared to hear them out. Before Jax could start explaining their purpose, Dr Jimenez interjected, "We've actually met before, Jax. It was a long time ago in Makati. I was invited by your parents for afternoon tea at your apartment. You and Digger had just come home from school when we were introduced. I don't expect you to remember that. Now, how can I assist you?"

CHAPTER FOUR

"I understand you were involved in Henry's last expedition. We're here to investigate it ... um..." Jax stammered, her nerves apparent.

Seeing her struggle, Doc stepped in. "Dr Jimenez, Jax and Digger are here to find out about their father's disappearance."

"As they should," Jimenez said, a response that took Doc by surprise.

She stood up, a petite figure, and walked over to her desk. Picking up her phone, she scrolled through it briefly before handing it to Jax. "This photo came from Henry's satellite phone, the last time he contacted me. It's a bit fuzzy because of a storm; the signal was weak."

Jax scrutinized the photo. It seemed to show some ancient ruins, possibly in Central America. Dr Jimenez prompted her, "Zoom in, tell me what you see in the shadows of those ruins."

With Digger peeking over her shoulder, Jax zoomed in on the image. "It ... looks like someone."

"Wait," Digger said, taking the phone. He adjusted the contrast. "There, it's clearer ... there's definitely a person, a girl, and..." He looked up at Jimenez, his expression one of disbelief, "She's wearing a headdress ... she looks like a bird!"

Jax examined the photo again, seeing the same figure, then passed the phone to Doc. "See her?" she asked.

"Yeah, but could be just a local, right?" Doc remarked.

Jimenez explained, "She is local, but not in the way you think. The headdress design is specific to a Nahuati, 'Precious Feather Flower,' an Aztec goddess of fertility and fresh water."

"Fresh water ... like the Surigao River's source," Digger connected.

"The Diwata Mountains," Jax added, piecing things together.

Jimenez nodded. "Exactly where Henry disappeared, shortly after taking this photo. It supports his theory that Aztecs fled there in 1530, hiding in the rainforest. The locals have always been scared of the Diwatas, the birdmen. Henry was the one who figured out the connection."

"And you were the only one who believed him," Jax observed.

Jimenez sighed, "It took a lot to convince me, but after Cindy vanished there four years earlier, Henry was driven to prove his theory—that she was taken by an Aztec birdman."

Doc, intrigued, asked, "What's with the bird imagery, though?"

"Quetzalcoatl, the feathered serpent and Aztec creator god," Jimenez explained. "In 1520, when Cortés journeyed overland to Tenochtitlan, now known as Mexico City, he was perceived as Quetzalcoatl by King Moctezuma, fulfilling a prophecy."

Doc shifted focus. "Do you have a triangulation of Henry's satellite phone?"

"No," Jimenez replied, "Henry insisted on total blackout. Only Ito Santos knew Cindy's last GPS location. It was because of…"

"Rafe Maddox," Jax interjected with a hint of disdain.

"Yes, I gather Tilly or Des told you about him. 'Rafe,' old Norse for 'wolf', quite fitting for him."

"So, you don't know exactly where Henry disappeared?" Doc pressed.

"The search team needed a precise location, but…" Jimenez trailed off.

"We've got Henry's diary," Jax began, hopeful.

"It was found with Ito," Jimenez admitted, revealing another piece of the puzzle.

Digger was puzzled. "Wasn't Ito lost with Dad?"

"No, no, Ito's body was found far from the Diwata Mountains. The police think he was trying to get help. He nearly made it to Upper Libas," Jimenez said sombrely.

"How did he die?" Jax asked.

"He likely capsized his canoe and hit his head. The diary was in the canoe, along with this…" Jimenez stood up, walked to a cabinet, and returned with a well-worn Australian Army slouch hat. Handing it to Digger, she said, "It's your father's. He was known for it. You should have it."

Doc, still focused on the mission, asked, "Would Ito's wife know the GPS location?"

"There's a possibility … when Ito was lost, so was the family income, there are eight kids … they're very tight-lipped about it. Jimenez's tone turned urgent. "If you're thinking of visiting them, do it quickly. If Maddox gets there first, there's no telling what he'd do to get that location."

Doc was puzzled. "But he's had plenty of time to do that."

"Not exactly," Jimenez clarified. "The diary has only surfaced a while ago and some of the pages were photographed by the officer who had it. I know for a fact he sold those pages to Maddox in Manila only two weeks ago … He's likely on the same trail as you."

It took an hour for them to drive to the small village of Tula, west of Davao City. As they entered the village, a few kilometres off the highway, the contrast was stark: from the first-world environment of Davao City to the third-world reality of Tula, where poverty was evident. Doc and Jax, accustomed to village life from their time in Kota Kinabalu, found this place distinctly different. The thatched-roof houses might have been similar, but the air of despair among the residents was palpable.

"These people are doing it tough," Digger commented from behind the steering wheel.

From the back seat, Jax chimed in, "Christina said to find the Barangay police. One of them is Ito's son, and he'll take us to the family home."

Navigating through kids, animals, and potholes filled with brown water, Digger pulled up outside a small police station. A cop was just about to enter the building when Jax quickly rolled down her window and called out to him, "Excuse me … Officer…"

He stopped and walked over to the car. Jax stepped out, preferring a face-to-face talk. "My name is Jax de Loite. Dr Christina

Jimenez from the Davao Museum said Officer Juno Santos is stationed here."

The young officer, in his early twenties, grinned. "That's me. I think I know your name. Are you related to Sir Henry?"

As Digger joined them, sporting his dad's hat, Juno's eyes shone. "You are, that's his hat," he exclaimed.

"We're his kids. This is Digger," Jax introduced.

Digger and Juno shook hands.

After a quick chat, Juno hopped in the car with them and led them through the village to his family's house. On the way, he told the story of his dad's discovery.

"I was part of the search team. We got a tip from a missionary that a local found a canoe near Libas village, on the Surigao River. When we got there, we only found that hat in the canoe. Two days later, we found my dad's body on the riverbank. My bosses said he hit his head on a rock and died. Here we are. Just park here."

Stepping out of the car, they saw a scene totally different from the rich areas they just left. "That must have been awful, finding your dad like that. I'm really sorry for you and your family," Jax said, offering her condolences.

"I am now the sole breadwinner for my family," he explained, shooing away chickens and dogs as he led them to the front door. He paused at the entrance. "Please, give me a moment to speak with my mother. She's very private and easily upset."

"Certainly," Jax agreed.

As he disappeared inside, they stood on the porch, surveying the dire living conditions of the family. Jax noticed something and glanced back at the house; three young boys peeked at her from a window, ducking away when she spotted them. Jax couldn't help but giggle.

"They've probably never seen the likes of us before," Doc remarked, "not out here in the boondocks."

The door swung open, and Juno ushered them inside.

The interior was spartan. A small, weather-worn woman stood to greet them, flanked by four children on either side, two teenage girls, and six boys ranging from four years old to Juno's age, and one next to Juno who was seventeen. Juno introduced them, saving his mother Gina for last. She then gestured for them to sit at the dinner table while the two girls fetched snacks. Jax's eyes welled up with tears, moved by the family's generosity despite their poverty.

Juno explained, "Mother doesn't speak much English, so I will translate for her."

Jax glanced at Digger, who respectfully had taken off his hat. He gave a nod, signalling her to continue. "First off, we're really sorry for what you're going through. Tilly sent her best wishes too." At the mention of Tilly, a slight smile flickered on Gina's sad face, clearly grateful for Tilly's financial help. Jax pulled out an envelope from her jacket and handed it to Gina. "My family wants you to have this, to help in these tough times."

Gina opened the envelope to find ten thousand US dollars, and tears instantly filled her eyes. She spoke quickly to Juno, who translated, "She's overwhelmed ... she's never seen this much money before. This means she can move and make sure the kids get a good education. I was the only one who went to school because Dad worked for Sir Henry. We used to live in Davao, but had to move here after Dad died. Davao was too expensive."

"Even though we've never met, we've always thought of you as family. We hope this money helps you start over," Jax said. "There's something we need to ask, Gina. It's really important to us ... Is there anything of Ito's that could help us find where my dad disappeared?"

Gina looked nervously at Juno. "A foreigner was here yesterday, asking the same thing. He wanted to buy Dad's stuff. Mum sold him an old phone that doesn't work anymore."

"Was this guy's name Maddox, by any chance?"

"We're not sure; he didn't give his name. He communicated in our language through his three companions. I wasn't here to interpret. Mum says they didn't seem trustworthy. He was adamant about buying the phone, even paid five hundred US dollars for it. We couldn't figure out why."

"Is that all he bought?"

"Yep, nothing else."

"No maps, books, or letters?" Jax pressed on. "How did Ito keep in touch with Henry in Manila?"

"Dad had a phone from him. It was updated every year, but there are spots with no signal. It worked well in Davao, but not here."

"And the latest phone?"

"That's a puzzle; it wasn't found with him."

"What about the older phones, like from around 2003?" Jax mused, thinking they might hold key info about her mum's disappearance.

"Those phones were just for contacting your dad or organising trips. Each year, your dad told mine to sell the old one and keep the money. Then he'd send a new one."

"Smart," Doc chimed in. "Henry was keeping all communication under wraps. He must've been really wary of something, or someone."

Jax felt a tinge of disappointment, realising they needed the GPS data to make a case for an expedition to find Henry. She wondered if the phone sold to Maddox had that vital info.

CHAPTER
FIVE

There was silence in the car on the way to drop Juno off at the police station. Jax gazed out of the window at the setting sun, pondering if embarking on the mission had been a colossal mistake.

Unlike the disheartened Jax and Digger, Doc, still optimistic, asked Juno, "I'm sorry to have to ask this, but is there any chance I can see the police and coroner's report for Ito?"

"Yes, I have it all at the station. What are you looking for?"

"I'm not sure, maybe something overlooked."

Shortly after, Juno escorted Doc into the station, leaving Digger and Jax in the car. After ten minutes, Doc re-emerged, signalling them to come inside.

The room contained three desks and a holding cell. Juno introduced Jax and Digger to his boss, a stocky man with a noticeable gut, as Barangay Captain Del Rosario.

At Juno's desk, Doc was scrutinizing a computer screen. "Check this out," he invited them.

Crowded around the monitor, they saw a harrowing crime scene photo: Ito lying by the riverbank.

"Oh no, poor Ito," Jax whispered sadly.

"Can I get a copy of this photo?" Doc asked. Captain Del Rosario, heaving himself up, shuffled over. After glancing at the screen, he gave a nod. "Sure, why not." Doc handed over a USB stick.

Later, back in their Davao hotel room, Doc, laptop perched on his knees, plugged in the USB. Across from him, Jax and Digger sat, nursing beers, their faces showing the strain of the day.

"There was a detail I couldn't talk about back at the station," Doc began, turning his laptop towards them. The grim image of Ito by the riverbank popped up again, zoomed in on his right hand. It was clear something was scrawled in the mud. "I think he used his index finger to write this before he died. Looks like '7.8232, 126.1769' to me."

Digger leaned in, squinting. "It's a bit unclear, but I see it. What do those numbers mean?"

"My hunch? GPS triangulation coordinates."

Jax almost leaped in surprise. "What!"

"I reckon our friend Ito left us directions," Doc said, smiling broadly.

Jax and Digger, utterly astonished, looked at each other. Digger slapped Doc's hand in a low five. "Ito, what a legend!"

Rafe Maddox, a large man with a square jaw and features unattractive by Western standards, was incensed. He bellowed in a Brooklyn accent at the smaller man delivering the message, "What do you mean the phone had nothing on it!"

"Sir, it was wiped clean."

"That's what two-thousand pesos of my money bought me? Nothing!" he raged.

"He offered to exchange the phone," the man replied timidly.

This response only fuelled Maddox's anger. Seizing the messenger by the shirt front, he loomed over him menacingly. "Tell him he'll pay four-thousand pesos, cash, right now for the phone ... or I'll pay him a personal visit."

The messenger scuttled out of the room hastily. Maddox slumped into his chair, seething, glaring at his subordinate who sat silently across from him, wisely keeping quiet.

"What are you staring at?" Maddox snapped.

"Nothing, boss," the Filipino replied in a raspy voice. "He'll get the four-thousand, you can count on it."

"That's not what's eating at me. We've still got no lead ... I need those GPS coordinates. Someone's got them, I know it," Maddox growled, his frustration evident.

"But boss, it's useless. It's the place of the Diwatas, the birdmen. Nobody dares go there ... it's what happened to de Loite," the subordinate cautioned.

"That's just mumbo jumbo," Maddox dismissed. "When Tito gets back, we're paying the Barangay police in Tula another visit."

"What for? They already told us they know nothing," his subordinate pointed out.

"If your contacts had squeezed Ito, like I instructed, Bato, before they killed him, we'd have those coordinates."

"What could the cops have? They had nothing last time we were there," Bato grumbled.

"I dunno ... but if anyone else is sniffing around for the same thing, I wanna find out. I heard there were three foreigners at the Davao Museum this morning meeting with Jimenez. Take it from me, that ain't no accident."

When Jax got to her hotel room, she spotted the message light blinking. A voicemail from Juno was waiting: "Hey, after you split, we took a closer look at the photo I passed to you and spotted something. Zoom in on papa's finger, and you'll see he scribbled something in the mud; the numbers 7.8232, 126.1769 or 1759 —can't tell which. Captain Del Rosario reckons they're GPS coordinates. Call me back."

Those numbers made them sitting ducks, exactly what Doc wanted to dodge. Juno had left his number, so Jax rang him up right away. Past 7 pm, and she hit voicemail; the station was closed. Jax hung up, a ball of worry about their safety. She needed to clue in Digger and Doc.

"No landline at the Santos' and Juno was off-grid, no cell... what now?" Jax said.

"No sweat, I'll zip over and give Juno the heads-up, no need for the whole crew to roll out," Digger offered, leaning against his doorway. Across the hall, Doc chimed in, "You sure? I'm okay to make the trip with you."

"Nah, you and Jax get cracking on the expedition plan. I don't need to be in that mix. Back in an hour, tops."

Jax, standing in the hallway, nodded. "Cool, hit us up if things go south ... well, you'll need to scout for a signal..."

"Go to the station with Juno and call us from there." Doc said.

"Good thinking," Jax agreed.

"No drama, I'll head out now. Might grab a bite on the way."

Jax gave him a quick, gentle peck on the cheek. "Stay sharp, bro." She pivoted to Doc, "How about the coffee shop downstairs in ten?"

Doc nodded, "Make it fifteen. Gotta shower first."

The drive to Tula was brutal for Digger, especially with the heavens opening up. It wasn't just raining; it was an absolute downpour. He leaned closer to the windshield, straining to see the road as the wipers struggled against the relentless sheets of water. Things got even hairier when he veered off the highway; the rain had turned the dirt track to Tula into a pothole minefield, and in the murky glow of the headlights, spotting the axle-breakers was a game of chance.

He rolled into Tula in one piece, but it had taken way longer than he'd planned. His headlights washed over the Santos house, revealing another vehicle out front. Killing the lights, he pulled up and, with the rain letting up a bit, dashed for the shelter of the house's eaves. Shouts from inside caught his ear. Sneaking a glance through a window, he saw Juno tied to a chair, face swollen and bruised. A stocky Filipino was standing over Juno, while a shorter, wiry one kept a pistol trained on him. The other family members were lined up against the wall, panic etched on their faces. Digger knew he had to act fast. He sprinted back to his car, executed a stealthy U-turn, and sped towards the village.

Pulling up at the police station, he bolted out and made for the door, finding it deserted. An emergency number was posted on the door, but his phone was dead, signal-wise. Driving back towards

Davao to pick up a signal wasn't an option—time was too tight. In a snap decision, he booted the door open. Inside, he found a card on the captain's desk, grabbed the desk phone, and dialled. Captain Del Rosario answered, and Digger quickly briefed him on the situation. The instruction was to wait.

Moments later, a vehicle pulled up, and Del Rosario's imposing figure filled the doorway. "How many?" he demanded.

"Two," Digger replied, urgency in his voice.

"Foreigners?"

"No."

"Alright, let's hit it. You're with me." Digger hopped into the police ATV, Del Rosario driving them towards the Santos house, lights flashing. "Check the glove box," the captain ordered.

Inside, Digger found a holstered .38. "You good with this?"

The ATV screeched to a halt right by the SUV outside the Santos house, its bull bar just shy of ramming it. Digger was impressed with Del Rosario's precision. The captain leapt out, gun at the ready, and charged towards the front door. Digger was right on his heels. They took positions on either side of the door. Del Rosario bellowed in Cebuano, demanding the assailants come out with their hands up.

CHAPTER
SIX

The situation was a textbook Mexican standoff. Digger and Del Rosario exchanged looks of sheer helplessness after hearing the response from inside. Digger didn't need to know Cebuano to understand the dire implications.

"He's going to blast them all, isn't he?" Digger muttered under his breath.

"Yes, starting with Juno. We've only got one option," Del Rosario replied, his voice heavy with resignation. He then yelled in English, "I'm alone! Let me in unarmed, and then you can leave. No-one gets hurt. Deal?"

A chilling silence hung in the air. Del Rosario subtly signalled towards the side of the house, mimicking a gun with his fingers. Digger got the message—hide and then take the shot. His heart pounded at the thought; he'd never aimed a gun at someone before.

The door slowly opened.

Following Del Rosario's silent instruction, Digger stealthily moved to the side of the house, staying out of sight.

Del Rosario, gun in hand but raised in surrender, stood in the doorway. Digger overheard the voice inside demanding the captain drop his gun.

Clutching his own weapon, Digger aimed with shaky hands. Suddenly, the icy touch of a gun barrel pressed against the back of his head, and the distinct sound of a trigger cocking filled his ears. A gruff voice, tinged with a Brooklyn accent, barked, "Drop it, and hands up. You too, sheriff, or your buddy here gets it."

Trapped, both Digger and Del Rosario had no choice but to comply.

Jax glanced at her phone again, a knot of worry forming in her stomach.

Doc, sitting across from her, noted her unease. "Getting close to panic time?"

"Yes," Jax admitted, her voice laced with concern. "Something's off ... I can feel it."

Doc had learned the hard way to trust her instincts; they had an uncanny track record. "Well, there's not much to do except maybe rent another car and head to Tula."

"Let's give him another half hour. If we haven't heard anything by then, that's exactly what we'll do."

The half hour whizzed by. With determination, Jax rose from her seat and made a beeline for the concierge to sort out a car. Doc trailed behind, settling the coffee shop bill. Plans for their expedition had been put on the back burner, overtaken by Jax's sixth sense.

Just as Jax approached the concierge desk, her phone buzzed. She snatched it from her pocket, anxiety in her eyes. "Hello?" she answered, not recognising the number.

"I'll only say this once, de Loite. Yeah, I know who you are. You met with Jimenez's this morning, and Henry's hat's hard to miss. Lucky for you, your brother's still breathing. But if you keep poking around for Henry, you might not be so lucky next time. Got it? Leave in the morning. I've got the numbers: 7.8232, 126.1759." The line went dead.

Doc arrived just in time to see the blood drain from Jax's face. "Was that...?" he began, then noticed her pallor. "What happened?"

"That was Rafe Maddox. He's got Digger and the GPS numbers – 7.8232, 126.1759. He's threatening to shoot Digger unless we bail from Davao," she said, her voice tinged with despair.

Doc folded his arms and fixed her with a serious look. "Okay, first off, Digger or Juno gave him the wrong GPS. It's 1769, not 59. That's a difference of 10 degrees. Digger knew that and bought us some time."

"You're suggesting we ignore the threat?"

"You bet. Do you really think he'll let Digger go after he finds the location? I don't think so."

They stood there, eyes locked, each weighing the potential consequences. Colour slowly returned to Jax's cheeks as a fierce resolve took root. Then, with a steely edge in her voice, she snarled, "Let's do it."

Back in her hotel room, Jax called Carter to update him. Carter was seriously worried about Maddox holding Digger, and possibly Juno, hostage. He insisted that risking their lives wasn't an option and ordered Jax to immediately contact the police. Jax stood frozen by the window, gazing blankly at the bay, her mind a whirlwind of decision-making. Should she follow orders? No, that would only give Maddox more time, putting Digger in deeper danger. Could they beat Maddox to the right coordinates and confront them? No chance, they lacked the weapons and skills. Then, a name popped into her mind: Dr Jimenez. She knows Maddox, helped Henry's previous expeditions ... she'll have the answers. Jax quickly dialled her number. Jimenez picked up, and before Jax could explain, cut in.

"I'm close to your hotel. Let's meet in the coffee shop in ten minutes. It's better not to talk over the phone."

Jax then rang Doc. It was 11 pm, and he was lounging in bed watching a movie.

In the coffee shop, Jax and Doc awaited Jimenez. She arrived looking stunning, her hair up, dressed in a striking crimson dress.

"Wow, Doctor, did I pull you away from dinner with the president?" Jax joked.

Jimenez chuckled as she sat. "Call me Christina. Your call saved me from a tedious government event, for which I'm eternally grateful. Now, what's going on?"

After they filled her in, Christina's expression turned grave. "This is serious ... Rafe Maddox is dangerous ... I've been trying to nail him for years. But he's got connections in high places, making him almost untouchable. Your boss is right; you can't risk Digger's life."

Jax's heart sank, their expedition seeming increasingly impossible. But then Christina's eyes lit up. "Hold on, I know a mercenary who'd jump at this. He's been itching to get at Maddox for ages. Plus, he's worked with your father before. I'll contact him first thing in the morning. Hopefully, he's in Davao. At 9 am, you need to call the Tula police station…"

"What about Juno and the Santos family? Could Maddox have taken Juno too?" Doc asked.

"The Tula police will know, or they'll find out," Christina assured. Standing up, followed by Doc and Jax, she added, "I can't promise not to worry, but try to rest. Tomorrow's a big day."

As Christina readied to leave, Jax caught Doc's admiring glance. Teasingly, she extended her hand for a handshake. "Thank you, Christina. Without you, we'd be totally lost."

Once Christina had left, Jax nudged Doc playfully. "Got a soft spot for older women, huh?"

Doc flashed a grin at Jax. "I'm drawn to strong women, age doesn't matter."

Jax lay on her back in bed, eyes fixed on the ceiling, unable to sleep. The full moon cast a spell of dancing shadows that, to her imagination, took on the forms of various animals. A tiny light, resembling a firefly, flickered at the foot of her bed, captivating her. Was she dreaming or awake? As she watched, a distant sound of a didgeridoo began to emerge, growing louder and clearer as it seemed to draw nearer. It crescendoed with a sharp, percussive clap of sticks, causing her to flinch. In that moment, the firefly's glow burst forth into a vivid, colourful birdman figure, commanding the room with an intense, eagle-like stare. Then, as the didgeridoo's rhythm started anew, the birdman's shape shifted, morphing into the familiar form of Digger.

"He's got Juno and me, Jax…" Digger's image conveyed urgently. "I overheard him—they're planning a chopper pick-up tomorrow, to take us to Upper Libas… I, I…"

Abruptly, the didgeridoo fell silent, and the ghostly image of Digger vanished as if it had never been. Jax's eyes snapped open to the reality of her room, sunlight streaming through the curtains. She checked her bedside clock—6 am. It was clear to her that Digger had reached out through her Dreaming, providing crucial insight. Without hesitation, she grabbed her phone and dialled Doc.

Doc had long since stopped questioning Jax's Dreaming experiences. This time, it seemed entirely plausible that she'd have such a connection with Digger. The insight from the Dreaming could be their ticket to outsmarting Maddox, provided they could find the means.

While having breakfast in the hotel café, Jax's phone buzzed. It was Christina. After sharing Digger's message, Jax listened to Christina's update. Finishing the call, Jax relayed to Doc, "We're to stay put. Christina's bringing Cal Christo to meet us."

"Cal Christo? Sounds like a musketeer," Doc joked, trying to inject some humour into the situation.

Half an hour later, Christina arrived, dressed casually in jeans and a T-shirt. She was accompanied by a man who was the complete opposite of what his name might suggest. Standing at an imposing 6'4", his military-style haircut and muscles almost bursting out of his army fatigues, he was the image of a seasoned soldier. His face, crisscrossed with scars, held an expression as steadfast as stone. Christina introduced him as Cal, who, with a solemn nod, extended a handshake that was as large as a baseball mitt.

As the briefing continued for twenty minutes, Cal's demeanour began to soften, revealing a surprisingly warm personality beneath his rugged exterior.

"You should call the Tula barangay captain for his opinion, but honestly, it's best if he stays out of this. His involvement could complicate things. I've got a couple of guys ... and I can arrange a chopper to drop us close to your GPS coordinates. Maddox won't expect that," Cal suggested.

"An ambush," Jax clarified. "How many can the helicopter take?"

"Just three, plus the pilot."

"That's not going to work. We'll need either two trips or a bigger chopper. We can't go ahead without everyone," Jax insisted.

"Birdman, I've scoured those jungles plenty, never came across any trace of them," Cal reflected. "Henry got obsessed with finding them after Cindy was taken. You reckon he found them?"

"Yes, I'm sure of it."

CHAPTER
SEVEN

After a long phone conversation with Captain Del Rosario, Jax had a clear picture of the kidnapping. She also had a detailed description of Maddox and his accomplices, along with the plate number of their vehicle. Del Rosario had already issued an all-points bulletin on the vehicle, but so far, there were no hits. Because a cop had been kidnapped, he had no choice but to inform the National Intelligence Coordinating Agency (NICA). He provided Jax with the contact details for Deputy General Nur Sidri in Davao. It was standard procedure for a task force to be assembled in kidnapping cases. Jax inquired about the Santos family; they'd had a scare but were okay.

Jax re-joined the others at the table in the hotel café and updated them.

"Leave dealing with the NICA to me. I've known Nur Sidri for years; it'll be about convincing him not to form a task force. They'd only slow us down," Cal explained. "What we need from them is a chopper, they have a bigger one than I can get."

Doc asked, "What about the APB?"

"Don't worry about that. Maddox would've ditched the car minutes after he left Tula. Our focus while prepping should be monitoring air movements to Upper Libas."

"My team can handle that," Christina chimed in.

"Great. Then I assume we can use your offices at the museum as our base?" Cal asked.

"Yes, we also have a helipad."

Both Jax and Doc were impressed by the efficiency of Cal and Christina.

"Now we need to tackle the challenging part," Cal said seriously, "deploying in the jungle."

In the pitch black, hogtied and gagged, Digger felt every jolt and bump from the trunk of the car. His only silver lining was that Maddox didn't speak Cebuano, so the conversation was in English. Although muffled, Digger managed to make out their words over the noise of the wheels on the dirt road.

Juno was in the back seat, also gagged, his wrists and ankles bound. His face bore the marks of the earlier assault at his home—a black eye, a split lip, and a cut eyebrow. He was less concerned about his injuries and more relieved that his family and Captain Del Rosario were safe.

"It was a mistake leaving that cop alive," grumbled the stocky guy beside Juno.

Maddox, sitting in the front passenger seat, swivelled his head around to glare at the hefty man. "Hari, if I want your advice—which I don't—I'll ask for it."

"I'm with Hari, boss. He'll have every cop in the region after us by now," added the scrawny driver.

Maddox faced forward again, growling at the driver. "You too, Bato. Just focus on driving. I'll handle the important stuff. I threw the cops a curveball ... they think we're heading to Upper Libas."

"So, where are we really going, boss?" Bato asked.

"To the source of the Enchanted River."

This revelation left Juno and Digger increasingly anxious. Maddox had thrown Del Rosario off the scent, and he, in turn, would've misled Jax. The rescue party was now chasing a ghost trail.

In the confines of the trunk Digger tried to meditate, hoping to send a message to his sister, but it proved impossible.

"I feel so helpless leaving everything to Cal," Jax confided to Doc in the elevator, on their way up to their hotel rooms.

"Yeah, but you're the hands-on type ... I get your anxiety. Just remember, Cal's a pro at this stuff," Doc reassured her.

"I should probably update Carter," Jax mused.

"Definitely, before he does something we don't need," Doc agreed.

Stepping out of the elevator, Jax dialled Carter, updating him on their situation. He wasn't thrilled about her disregarding his request but felt somewhat relieved knowing Cal was involved, recalling him from his days as editor of Eco Magazine in Manila.

"He's one tough mother that's for sure, and that's what you need against Maddox. But honestly, I'd feel better if you and Doc just headed home and left Cal and Dr Jimenez to handle it."

"No way, boss. We're here to finish a job," Jax firmly replied.

"I wouldn't expect any less from you, Jax. You're as head-strong as Henry. But be cautious with Maddox; he's ruthless."

Pocketing her phone, Jax was satisfied Carter had agreed to their plan. She paused at her door, turning to Doc. "We've got the go-ahead."

"Good," Doc acknowledged. "Catch you in the lobby in half an hour."

The car jerked to a stop, and after a few tense minutes, the trunk flew open. Blinded by the sudden burst of sunlight, Digger squinted against the harsh glare. A distorted silhouette emerged, a hand brandishing a knife slicing through the ties binding his ankles. He was then yanked out roughly. As his eyes adjusted, he stretched out his limbs, cramped from curling up in the foetal position for what seemed like hours, his body screaming in protest.

Hari, wielding the knife that had freed him, stood close by, while Bato had a gun on him. Maddox, with his imposing bulk, dragged Juno out of the car. Surveying his surroundings, Digger realised they were in a desolate clearing, encircled by dense jungle. Not a soul, vehicle, or building in sight. The isolation was ominous, the perfect spot for an execution, where bodies could be left, only to be devoured by wildlife, vanishing without a trace.

But then, a rhythmic thumping sound pierced the silence—whop, whop, whop. The unmistakable sound of helicopter blades slicing through the air offered a momentary sense of relief. They weren't going to be executed; this was their pickup spot.

As the helicopter touched down, Bato kept his gun aimed at them, while Maddox strode over to talk to the pilot. Hari busied himself, transferring three kitbags from the car to the chopper. Digger exchanged a glance with Juno, blinking reassuringly, trying to convey a sense of calm despite their dire situation.

Amidst the chaos, Digger's mind raced. He desperately needed to send a message to Jax through the Dreaming, but meditation, with its requirement for tranquillity and silence, was impossible for now.

He eyed the sun, estimating it was nearing midday. Calculating their flight time could be vital for Jax to locate them, but he needed a starting point, which he lacked. Their phones had been destroyed to prevent tracking.

Then, a realisation struck him. The helicopter must have logged a flight plan. His gaze fixed on the chopper, noting a Navy decal and the identifier 6-PTFG, which he committed to memory.

Jax found Doc in the lobby, chilling with his kitbag. They'd already signed out of the hotel.

"Bit ahead of schedule, huh? Christina said we'd roll out at noon," Doc observed, glancing over his sunnies. He caught the worried look on Jax's face. "You stressing about Digger?"

"Kinda. This Maddox guy sounds like bad news. Carter says he's a real piece of work," Jax replied, her voice tinged with concern. "Guess Maddox is keeping Digger and Juno around for some sort of leverage."

"We'll handle it, Jax," Doc said, trying to pump up her spirits.

Right then, a sleek black SUV rolled up. Cal hopped out, and they They tossed their bags into the back and climbed into the vehicle.

As they hit the road, Cal shared his thoughts. "So, we're heading straight to the coordinates you provided. It's a better plan than chasing after Maddox without any solid leads."

Jax was about to voice her concerns, but Cal interrupted her. "Listen, your brother and Juno are Maddox's leverage right now. He won't harm them. He's just using them to wriggle out of a tight spot or to get his hands on something valuable."

Jax's expression showed her scepticism, and Cal noticed. "I get it, it's hard to accept. But you've got to trust me. When it comes down to it, it's us against them, and I'm fully committed to making sure we come out on top."

"Just... not at Digger and Juno's expense," Jax muttered, more to herself than anyone else in the car.

"We're doing everything we can to keep them safe. Got a call from Des Carter today—he's ready to support us with whatever we need," Cal reassured her.

"Cool," Doc joined in. "So, we're heading to the Davao Museum next?"

Jax, lost in her thoughts, gazed out the window.

"Yes. The chopper's picking us up from there in two hours. We need to be ready to go by then. I've got some high-tech satellite maps, and Christina's managed to get hold of a cutting-edge LiDAR map from some mining contacts. We'll use the next few hours to review them, plan our approach, and figure out the best spots for us to land and start searching."

CHAPTER EIGHT

Forty-five minutes into their flight, Digger gazed out at the vast sea of tropical treetops below. In the distance, partly veiled by clouds, was a mountain range. He didn't have a communication headset but was wearing noise-reducing earmuffs. The helicopter's side door was open, allowing a strong gust of wind to whip through the cabin, feeling almost like a powerful storm. Upfront, Maddox sat next to the pilot, appearing completely unbothered by the turbulence.

Digger could only catch bits and pieces of their conversation above the engine's loud hum. "Is that the Diwata Mountain range ahead?" Maddox yelled over to the pilot.

"Roger that … There are gold mining villages up there, I can…" the pilot began.

"No, follow the coordinates I gave you," Maddox instructed firmly.

"Understood … but finding a spot to land will be like a miracle," the pilot responded.

Digger's attention turned to the ground below. The dense jungle canopy seemed to consume everything, leaving no apparent space for a landing. Nevertheless, the helicopter began its descent, gliding over a slender river that glinted intermittently in the occasional sunlight breaking through the high clouds.

"That's your Enchanted River," the pilot called out to Maddox.

"We're looking for a waterfall…"

"There! Just ahead," the pilot pointed towards a clearing near a waterfall.

Maddox simply nodded, undaunted by the challenging terrain.

Skilfully, the pilot eased the chopper down into a small clearing next to a lagoon at the base of the fifty-metre-high waterfall.

Digger was struck by the sheer beauty of the scene. It was the quintessential image of a secluded waterfall in the heart of a lush tropical jungle.

As they watched the helicopter lift off and disappear into the sky, Digger took a moment to absorb the stunning environment. The exotic plants framing the clear blue lagoon, the vibrant symphony of the wilderness, and the powerful flow of the waterfall into the lagoon painted a scene straight out of Arthur Conan Doyle's 'The Lost World'. He half-expected a dinosaur to step out of the thick jungle, reminiscent of the book Henry had gifted him in his youth. Although set in the Amazon, the wild, untouched landscape around him felt eerily similar. The prospect of encountering the mythical Aztec birdmen in this ancient setting sent a chill of excitement through him. Yet, there was an unnerving feeling that unseen watchers were observing them from the dark embrace of the surrounding jungle.

The LiDAR maps Christina projected from her laptop onto the office wall displayed fascinating topography at the coordinates 7.8232, 126.1769.

"In archaeological research, these satellite maps are often overlooked by companies focused on mineral deposits. However, observe this area when zoomed in," Christina pointed out. "You can discern ruins in this mountain valley, arranged in a pattern consistent with Central American megalithic structures. It's likely what Henry was searching for."

The group was captivated. Without knowing it was the Diwata Mountains in Mindanao, one might have mistaken it for an ancient Aztec or Mayan site.

"Access is challenging. The dense jungle and rugged mountains necessitate rappelling from a helicopter," Christina analysed.

Doc, excited, chimed in, "We can manage that."

"Have either of you rappelled before?" Cal asked, a note of concern in his voice.

"No, but we can cut it," Jax asserted confidently.

Christina interjected with a dose of reality. "That's easier said than done, takes training."

Doc looked towards Cal. "Well, I figure we've got one of best instructors in the business. So let's not give it another thought, we're good to go, right, Jax?"

"Full-on," Jax responded with a smile and good old Aussie bravado.

Cal let out a light laugh. "Just make sure Carter doesn't find out about this. He wouldn't be impressed."

Cal turned his attention back to the map, contemplating their next steps. "We've got to be careful with the mountain weather—it's unpredictable. Wind conditions can turn treacherous during a rappel. I've done a few forest landings, and trust me, they're not without risks."

"If only we had this kind of detailed LiDAR mapping back in 2017. We might not have lost Henry," Christina said, a tone of regret in her voice.

"Or when my mum disappeared," Jax added, reflecting on the past.

"Looks like we're on the right track..." Christina started.

"And Maddox is chasing the wrong leads," Doc noted, piecing things together.

"Cal, any updates on chopper movements in that area today?" Christina inquired, looking for more information.

"Nothing's been reported. Maddox probably used military channels for communication, and those are out of our reach," Cal replied, providing an insight into their opponent's possible tactics.

"So, he could be on his way there or already be on-site," Doc speculated, considering the possibilities.

"Yes, but we need to keep our focus on our main goal," Cal emphasised, steering the group's attention back to their mission.

Jax, eager to proceed, asked, "Are we good to go?"

As if on cue, the sound of a helicopter landing on the helipad outside grabbed their attention.

Trudging through the dense jungle, Digger and Juno were tethered together, their wrists bound. Navigating the thick underbrush without being able to use their arms was a nightmare. Branches slapped their faces, and swarms of insects buzzed around, relentless and annoying. Thirsty, tired, and battered, they were pushed to their limits.

"We need a break," Digger called out to Maddox, who was leading the way, machete in hand. Maddox halted, his army shirt soaked in sweat.

"Okay, break for five," he commanded. "Give them water."

As Digger and Juno gratefully sipped from the offered water bottle, Hari kept watch, and Bato stepped into the bushes to relieve himself. Suddenly, Bato froze, his eyes fixed on a 1.5-metre green snake dangling from a branch right in his path.

"Whoa!" he yelled, drawing Maddox's attention. Maddox approached cautiously but stopped dead when he saw the snake.

"Don't move, Bato!"

"It's just a tree snake..." Bato started.

Juno, now standing, corrected him. "No, that's a Samar cobra."

Maddox snapped at Juno. "Shut it, or I'll gag you!"

Juno sat back down, muttering, "Okay, but it's a spitting cobra."

Hari looked puzzled. "A what?"

"A spitting cobra. It can spit venom up to two metres," Juno explained.

As Bato moved, the snake recoiled and lunged forward, spitting a stream of venom straight into his left eye. Bato's scream pierced the air as Maddox quickly decapitated the snake with his machete.

"My eye! It's burning!" Bato writhed on the ground in agony.

Maddox, desperate, turned to Juno. "Help him!"

"Untie me," Juno demanded, showing his bound wrists. "Without treatment, he'll be blind in an hour."

After a moment's hesitation, Maddox ordered, "Hari, untie him."

"Both of us," Juno insisted.

With a grumble, Maddox agreed. "Fine, both of them."

Hari cut their bonds, and Juno approached the still screaming Bato.

"You didn't have to kill the snake; it was just defending itself," Juno remarked.

"Just fix him!" Maddox growled.

Juno stood over Bato. "Stay still. I can prevent blindness, but you mustn't move."

Bato, his left eye swelling shut, nodded frantically.

Juno quickly unzipped his pants and relieved himself onto Bato's injured eye.

Maddox erupted, "What the hell are you doing?"

Juno calmly responded, "Urine can neutralise the venom. It has antiseptic properties."

While Juno diverted Maddox's and Hari's attention, Digger seized the moment. Quietly, he slipped away into the jungle's embrace, unseen.

Cal and two others, all decked out in army jungle fatigues, guided Jax and Doc towards the chopper, its rotors already spinning. A bit away, Christina struggled to keep her dress from billowing in the powerful downdraft.

As the helicopter ascended into the cloudy afternoon sky, Jax, now equipped with a helmet and communications gear, watched as Christina became a smaller figure on the ground below.

"Hey, how long's the flight?" Doc called out over the roar of the engine to the pilot.

"Forty minutes, if the weather cooperates," the civilian pilot responded.

Jax peered out the window, observing the ominous dark clouds with a trace of concern. Suddenly, a vision flashed in her mind—a message from Digger.

"Cal, Digger just sent me a telepathic message. A chopper with a Navy decal, identifier 6-PTFG. Does that mean anything to you?" she yelled to be heard over the noise.

Cal looked baffled. "You got what from who?"

"They've got this telepathic connection," Doc clarified.

Immediately, Cal turned to the pilot. "Can you check that out?"

The pilot switched channels and put through an inquiry. Soon enough, he confirmed that the helicopter in question was indeed Navy and had recently dropped off passengers in the upper Surigao River region, then returned to base. This information provided them with a vital clue: Maddox's drop-off point.

CHAPTER NINE

Hidden among the dense vegetation, Digger was lost in meditation, the resonant drone of a didgeridoo echoing his thoughts. Abruptly, Maddox's gruff voice shattered the tranquillity, severing his telepathic connection with Jax.

"Digger! I'm counting to ten. Show yourself or the kid cop gets it!"

Knowing he'd achieved his aim, Digger rose. "Chill, I'm here. Just needed to take a dump, that's all," he called out, casually strolling from the bushes, fastening his belt. He stopped, took off his slouch hat and wiping the sweat from his forehead asked Juno, "How's the patient, mate?"

"He'll make it," Juno replied, securing a makeshift bandage around Bato's head covering his left eye. "His eye's going to be out of action for a couple of days, though."

Maddox, clearly irritated, barked out, "Break's over. I wanna reach the mountains by nightfall. Move out!"

Juno assisted Bato to his feet, and the group set off again, trailing behind Maddox, who navigated with a GPS in one hand and a machete in the other.

The sky was ominous, and the mountain valley below them was engulfed in mist, making it challenging for the pilot to find a suitable spot to hover for the team's descent to the valley floor.

"We'll need to do a low rappel below 75 feet; our civvies haven't done it before," Cal informed the pilot.

"I'm concerned about that storm brewing. You know as well as I do that if a wind picks up in the valley, it could spell disaster."

"Yes, look, don't fret about the mist. Drop to the minimum anywhere in this valley; we'll manage from there."

"Roger that," the pilot concurred.

Cal turned to the others, "Prepare to rappel. Dino, you're first with the kitbags, followed by Jax, then Doc, Vehnee, and finally, me."

With the mission underway, Jax peered down at the mist-enshrouded valley below, her stomach twisting in knots.

Vehnee assumed the role of rappelling master, setting up the STABO rig from the rope gantry and anchor bar. He acquainted Jax and Doc with the harness before securely fastening it around Dino's waist and attaching the safety line. Both men were seasoned in the procedure. Dino secured the five kitbags with a tie, attaching it to his belt, then positioned himself in the doorway.

The helicopter descended steadily, buffeted occasionally by gusts from the looming storm. Time was of the essence. Jax and Doc sensed the urgency among the team.

Cal monitored the altimeter, and at 70 feet, he exchanged nods with the pilot, then signalled Vehnee with a thumbs-up. Vehnee patted Dino on the back, who stepped out of the helicopter without hesitation. The cabin filled with the loud whirring of the STABO rig, controlling Dino's descent into the mist.

When the rig began rewinding, Jax realised her turn had arrived. Vehnee guided her to the doorway, her nerves almost tangible. He secured the harness and safety to her as the clip locked onto the gantry.

Vehnee had to shout over the din of the engine and wind, "When you reach the ground, release both these clips for it to return for Doc, okay? You got that?"

"Yep, I can do it."

"Don't kick your legs, stay calm, you'll be fine. You have comms; if there's trouble, yell out."

She nodded.

He tapped her helmet, and with her eyes closed, she grasped the cable and stepped out into the void.

After a few seconds, she opened her eyes to the serene majesty of hanging in the sky, an exhilarating feeling despite the circumstances. A gust of wind swung her to an angle of about twenty or thirty degrees from the helicopter.

Inside, Vehnee alerted the team, "She's caught a gust and is off-centre! Should I abort?"

Doc peered down at Jax, who managed to give a thumbs-up.

"Continue, she's fine," Doc relayed, watching her descent into the fog.

The final thirty feet, navigating through branches, were the most challenging. Jax battled to avoid entanglement in the dense canopy.

Landing brought immense relief, only to be startled by hands quickly unclipping her from the safety and main lines. It was Dino, a reassuring presence.

Fifteen minutes later, the team regrouped on the ground, listening to the fading sound of the helicopter, now leaving them to their mission.

Thunder boomed off the mountains, and Maddox stopped hacking through the undergrowth to look up at the dark, moody sky. He checked his GPS. "We're still a few hours out from the coordinates."

"You wanted to hit the mountain range, and here we are," Digger pointed out, sounding a bit smug.

"Hey, watch it. I'm the one calling the shots here, remember? That storm's looking nasty. We gotta find someplace to crash for the night."

They were at the base of the mountains now, and the jungle was thinning out. The climb up was way easier than the trek through the thick jungle had been.

About twenty minutes later, they found a trail. Maddox stopped and said, "This looks like it cuts through a gorge into the valley. We'll take it at first light. For now, let's hunt for a cave to bunk in."

Not long after, Maddox hit the jackpot—a cave. They went in, causing a mega bat exodus. Hari, dodging bats left and right, backed right into this huge web with a giant huntsman spider, which freaked out and ended up in his hair.

"There's a massive spider on your head, Hari!" Bato yelled, peering through his one eye.

Juno, cool as a cucumber, went over to a frozen Hari, plucked the spider off him, and popped it back on its web. "Chill, it's just a huntsman. They're harmless."

"Yeah, easy for you to say," Hari muttered, looking a bit shaken but relieved.

Juno and Digger, both tough as nails, didn't even bat an eye at the bats or spider.

Maddox got busy setting up for the night. Just then, lightning zapped across the sky, followed by a thunderous boom that echoed all over the cave. The rain started hammering down like crazy. Talk about good timing—they'd found shelter just in the nick of time.

Digger and Juno stood at the cave's mouth, watching the rain pour down.

"This won't last," Juno said, feeling the cool breeze mixed with the rain. It was a nice break from the muggy air they'd been dealing with.

Juno was spot on; within an hour, the rain had stopped. The five of them huddled around a campfire, munching on the military rations Maddox had brought along.

"How far to the coordinates from here?" Bato quizzed Maddox.

"GPS says five kilometres, as the crow flies."

"And how sure are we this track will take us to the valley?" Digger chimed in.

"We're not, but where else is it gonna lead, right?" Maddox shrugged.

"So, what are we expecting to find there, boss?" Hari chimed in.

"Wouldn't mind a Macca's myself; this bully beef is wrong," Juno joked.

Even Maddox, usually unsmiling, cracked a grin. "We're looking for ruins. Henry de Loite, Digger's archaeologist dad, spent years searching Mindanao for an ancient temple."

"Did he find it?" Hari's eyes widened.

"I reckon he did ... ... Digger being here, wearing his dad's hat, kind of suggests it. But maybe something went south for him."

Hari's nerves kicked up a notch, like he was in the middle of a campfire ghost story. "Went south ... how?"

"It's more about 'what'... I'm guessing... a birdman," Maddox said with a sinister grin, clearly enjoying scaring Hari.

"A birdman!" Hari echoed, spooked. "The Diwatas?"

"The what?" Bato was clueless.

"You never heard of them?" Hari was surprised.

"Nope, I'm an Olongapo guy, remember?" Bato shrugged.

Juno explained, "Diwatas are mythical spirits in the Mindanao jungles, turning into birdmen with bright feathers..."

Bato was sceptical. "Come on, you're pulling my leg ... this is the 21st Century, man."

"It's legit," Maddox confirmed.

"Yeah," Digger added. "In 2003, a birdman took my mum. Dad witnessed it and kept returning here to find her. Then, in 2017, he and Juno's dad, Ito, disappeared too."

Juno nodded. "My dad and Henry uncovered lots of clues about the Diwata birdmen."

"I heard the same from my dad back in Manila. We even held a funeral with an empty casket since they never found their bodies."

"Where do these Diwatas hang out?" Bato was curious.

"Underground, like in caves..." Juno glanced around the dark cave.

Hari was properly freaked out now. "I don't want to meet them; they're devils."

"No," Digger corrected, "They're descendants of the Aztecs, survivors from when the Spanish conquered Mexico in 1519."

"How'd they end up here?" Bato wondered.

Maddox had the answer. "They were slaves on Spanish ships. When they first landed here, they were sent to gather supplies but bolted into the jungle instead. Found a hideout to keep up their Aztec ways."

"So what's in it for you, Maddox?" Digger asked.

Maddox grinned. "Aztec gold, my boy. Loads of it."

CHAPTER
TEN

As Cal directed his team into shelter, the sky opened up, drenching the landscape. They took refuge in a cavern large enough to fit two school buses side by side. While most of the group remained near the entrance, captivated by the downpour, Jax ventured deeper into the cave.

At the far end, she found a small waterfall pouring into a pond, with signs of ancient human activity around her, including primitive art on the cave walls. Doc soon joined her, drawn by curiosity.

"Find anything interesting?" he asked.

"Check out this cave art," Jax responded, casting her flashlight over the rugged wall.

Doc whipped out his iPhone 15 Pro Max, snapping pictures of the art, the waterfall, and then a shot of Jax beside the pond. He also snapped a selfie with her, with the waterfall as a backdrop.

"These will be great for Janet. Real field photos bring so much more to the narrative," Doc remarked, now recording video. "And I'm all set for power. Got a solar charger on my hat and four spare batteries."

"Ever the boy scout," Jax teased with a grin.

"I'm all for being prepared, but knots? That's where I struggle, especially untying them."

Cal arrived just as the rest of the team was busy setting up camp and getting a fire going. "We have a fresh water source then?" he noted, looking around.

Jax replied, "Might be the mysterious source of the Enchanted River."

"Enchanted River?" Doc echoed, intrigued.

"Yes," Jax affirmed. "The origin of the Surigao River, flowing from these mountains to the sea, has always been a mystery. That's why it's called the Enchanted River—this spot might be the source."

Doc, ever eager for a photo opportunity, suggested, "Sounds like the perfect spot for another selfie. Come on, Cal."

"No selfies for me, I prefer staying off the grid," Cal declined.

After snapping the selfie with Jax, Doc commented to her, as Cal moved away, "He's quite the mystery, isn't he?"

"Definitely makes it tough to create a solid story for the Next Files without him in it," Jax agreed, both of them pondering Cal's elusive nature.

In the depths of the cave, Jax was half-asleep in her sleeping bag, the distant echo of snoring reverberating off the stone walls. She tossed and turned, uneasy. Abruptly, she jolted awake—looming over her was the silhouette of a birdman, its presence eerie and unsettling in the dim light. Jax's heart pounded in her chest, a mix of fear and fascination gripping her: 'Is this real? A dream? A warning?' She lay frozen, too afraid to make a sound and alert the others.

In the faint light, she could barely make out Doc's sleeping form a few metres away, and further off, Cal, Vehnee, and Dino were shadows near the dwindling campfire. The birdman, with his intricate plumage, silently raised an arm, pointing ominously towards the cave wall behind the waterfall. Jax's eyes strained to pierce the darkness, but she saw only shadows and shapes that seemed to dance and shift.

When she dared to glance back, the birdman had vanished as if he were a phantom. Chills ran down her spine, and every sound in the cave seemed amplified in her heightened state of alert. With a mix of trepidation and exhaustion, she forced herself to lie back down, her mind racing with questions as she eventually slipped back into a restless sleep.

As the sun rose, Maddox was already on his feet. Hari, spooked by the night's thoughts of birdmen, spiders, snakes, and bats, hadn't slept a wink and was visibly irritable.

"Rise and shine, everyone," Maddox barked. Hari and Bato groaned in response, but Juno and Digger were up and ready. Juno leaned in towards Digger, "Hear anything from ... you know who?"

Digger knew he was asking about Jax and any dream messages. "Nothing. Radio silence," he replied in a low tone.

"That's enough chit-chat," Maddox interjected. "Gear up, we're moving out, now."

"What about breakfast?" Juno asked, a bit cheekily.

Maddox gave him a stern look, one eyebrow raised.

"I'll take that as a 'no'," Juno murmured to himself.

Leading the way out of the cave, Maddox stretched in the morning sunlight, appreciating the beauty of the jungle and clear blue skies. Digger joined him, dusting himself off with his hat.

"Was the hat all they found of Henry?" Maddox queried.

"Just his diary, and no, you didn't get a mention in it," Digger responded.

"That's disappointing. After all our run-ins, I thought I'd at least be his Moriarty or something," Maddox growled.

"Maybe that was too personal, even for his diary."

"I was at the burial, you know. Saw your sister and the maid in the rain, an empty casket being lowered. Where were you?"

"Up in North Queensland, tracing my roots."

"What did you find?"

"My way here. And you? Why were you at my father's grave?"

Maddox took a moment before replying, "I was in Manila, heard about his disappearance. Saw the obituary and decided to pay my respects to an old rival. Didn't know about the empty casket till later."

As Hari, Bato, and Juno gathered, Maddox gave a nod. "Alright, let's get moving."

As soon as Jax woke, she remembered her visitation and jumped up to check where the birdman had pointed. Now with daylight aiding her, she noticed something behind the waterfall. Grabbing her torch, she directed the beam towards the hidden spot. Doc, already awake, joined her in examining it, while Cal, Vehnee, and Dino prepared to leave.

"What's up, Jax?" Doc asked, curious.

"I had a visit last night from a birdman. He pointed at the waterfall. I looked there, and when I looked back at him, he'd gone," Jax explained, her voice tinged with bewilderment.

"Real or a dream?" Doc wondered aloud.

Shining her torch on something intriguing, Jax said, "Not sure, but look, there's definitely something behind this waterfall."

"We should tell Cal," Doc quickly suggested, and went to bring him. As they all gathered, Doc relayed Jax's experience, everyone's interest now on the waterfall.

Jax continued trying to see through the cascade. "I can't see it clearly," she admitted.

Without hesitation, Jax stepped into the pond and waded under the waterfall. She emerged on the other side, completely drenched but filled with excitement. "You've got to see this!" she called out.

Following her lead, Doc hurried through the waterfall. Cal, a bit more reserved, told Vehnee and Dino, "Wait here, guys." He then cautiously followed Jax and Doc.

On the other side, Cal found Doc and Jax, her torch revealing a long, narrow, dark tunnel.

"What the...?" Cal exclaimed, surprised.

Jax, filled with excitement, insisted, "The birdman was leading us to this tunnel. We have to explore it."

The track through the gorge was a spectacle of nature's power, scarred by years of landslides that had strewn massive boulders and debris across their path. Their progress was slow and fraught with challenges.

After hours of strenuous effort, the group reached a precipice. They were greeted by the vast expanse of a hidden valley cradled by the mountains. They stood in awe, taking in the breathtaking scene.

"How are we going to get down there?" Hari asked, his voice laced with a tremble of apprehension.

"We need to be birdmen," Juno joked sarcastically.

Hari, his superstitions getting the better of him, quickly genuflected, convinced of the evil nature of birdmen.

"There, look..." Maddox pointed out a narrow track clinging to the cliff face, a precarious ribbon winding its way down.

Hari's eyes widened in terror. "You're not thinking we follow that down there!" he gasped, freaked.

"I sure am," Maddox replied firmly, his voice brooking no argument.

"No way, man. That track's only two feet wide ... there's nothing to hold onto ... it's suicide..." Hari's voice was thick with panic.

Maddox faced him squarely, "Think of it this way, Hari. You either follow the track with us or we leave you here for the birdmen, snakes, and spiders."

Hari, caught between two fears, hesitated before nodding in a resigned agreement, sweat beading on his forehead.

Maddox didn't hesitate. He stepped onto the narrow trail, skilfully navigating the treacherous descent. Digger and Juno followed suit, demonstrating similar confidence. Bato, hindered by his partial sight, and Hari, with his bulk, found the going tough. The path allowed for only one foot in front of the other.

"Don't look down..." Maddox's warning echoed back to them.

Hari, unable to resist, glanced down and his heart lurched at the sheer drop, a chasm of over 1,000 feet, the valley below hidden by clouds.

Further along, the track became even more perilous. A section of the cliff face overhung the path, forcing them to duck. Hari balked, his large frame struggling to fit. Bato caught up to him, realising the dilemma.

"You alright, Hari?" he asked, trying to sound calm.

Hari, shaking uncontrollably, mumbled, "No, no, I've got vertigo."

"It's acrophobia you've got, not vertigo. That's dizziness," Digger called back, hoping to ease his fear.

"No, it's vertigo ... everything's spinning," Hari insisted, his face ashen, his eyes wide with terror.

As Hari began to wobble, Bato reached out to steady him. Digger, realising the peril, shouted, "No! Don't grab him, or you'll both go over!"

But in that heart-stopping moment, Hari's foot slipped. He dangled precariously, Bato clinging desperately to his arm. Digger knew it was a dire situation. "Let him go, mate," he urged Bato gravely.

In a final act of self-sacrifice, Hari locked eyes with Bato. With a decisive jerk, he freed his arm from Bato's grasp and plummeted into the abyss. His terrified scream echoed faintly as he vanished into the clouds below.

CHAPTER ELEVEN

The tunnel's slippery slope and pitch-black darkness, illuminated only by Cal's torch, made for a challenging descent. It was a narrow, single-file passage with a low ceiling, forcing everyone but Jax to stoop to avoid hitting their heads.

"Is this tunnel man-made?" Jax asked, looking up at Doc who was hunched over like Groucho Marx.

"No, judging by the walls, it seems to be an ancient volcanic vent, a passage for magma to reach the Earth's surface. This mountain range is probably riddled with them," Doc speculated.

"So we could easily get lost down here, like a labyrinth?" Jax pondered, a hint of concern in her voice.

"You're not wrong," Doc replied.

Reaching an intersection, Cal paused, turning to address the group. "This is exactly what Jax was talking about. Which way now? Both tunnels lead in different directions."

Jax flashed her torch around, searching for a clue. Her light stopped on an arrow etched deep into the wet rock floor. "Check this."

"I think you have a special connection here, Jax. You should lead," Cal suggested, acknowledging her intuition.

Without hesitation, Jax stepped into the left tunnel indicated by the arrow.

About an hour later, they entered a massive cavern adorned with enormous crystals, stalactites, and stalagmites. The sight was breathtaking—crystals as tall as four-storey buildings and as wide as the length of a baseball bat, some extending twelve metres from the ground and over a metre in width.

"These are selenite crystals, larger than the ones discovered in Mexico. They must be over five hundred thousand years old," Doc exclaimed in awe.

However, the beauty of the cavern was countered by its intense heat.

Cal checked a device. "It's 47.1 degrees Celsius in here. We need to leave, right now."

Doc, capturing the moment on his iPhone, fell behind. By the time he caught up, they were all visibly suffering from the heat.

"We're dehydrating fast, Jax. Find us a way out," Cal urged, his voice strained.

The natural fluorescence of the crystals bathed the cavern in light, aiding Jax in her search for an exit. She enlisted Doc's help to climb atop a large, toppled crystal, gaining a vantage point for a 360-degree view of the cavern. "There's a way out up here," her voice echoed.

Soon, they all managed to clamber onto the crystal, following Jax across another angled crystal to a hole in the cavern ceiling. Cal boosted Jax up to the manhole-sized opening, and one by one, they squeezed through to the other side.

Relief washed over them in the cooler air of the new chamber, complete with fresh running water and another tunnel at the far end. Refreshed by the clean spring water, they followed Jax into the next phase of their adventure.

Since the tragic loss of Hari, they had continued their descent, carefully navigating the narrow, serpentine path down the cliff face. Maddox, always a few steps ahead as the leader, rounded a corner and momentarily disappeared from view. When Digger and the others finally caught up, they were confronted with a sight that took their breath away.

Maddox stood before a fragile rope bridge that stretched across a fifty-metre-wide gorge. Far below, a river raged, its rapids a white blur two hundred metres down. The bridge, constructed of ancient, braided vines, hung precariously, swaying gently in the breeze. Four separate strands of vine spanned the gap.

The group gathered, eyeing the bridge warily, each pondering how to tackle this new obstacle.

Juno broke the silence. "There's a bridge like this near my village. It's shorter, but the technique's the same. You walk on the lower vines, holding the upper ones under your armpits for balance. Got it?"

Maddox, a hint of sarcasm in his tone, replied, "Easy for someone who's five foot nothing."

"Well, we're not getting across by just looking at it," Digger said, stepping onto the lower ropes. He followed Juno's instructions, crossing the bridge with cautious, shaky steps.

Maddox was about to follow when Juno held him back. "Wait, only one at a time. This old thing won't hold two. Be patient."

Once Digger reached the opposite side, Maddox took his turn. It was a slow, nerve-wracking process, but one by one, they each made their way across.

After fifteen intense minutes, they all stood on the far side, visibly relieved and bolstered by their triumph over another perilous hurdle in their quest.

✕

Cal checked his GPS, announcing, "We're at 7.8232, 126.1760."

Doc, standing nearby, asked, "So, nine minutes to our destination at 1769. How far is that?"

"About nine kilometres," Cal replied.

Jax, joining the conversation, queried, "In which direction?"

"West," Cal confirmed, turning to face the direction and pointing at a wall while reading the bearing from his device.

He then turned to face the tunnel, "Hmm, this tunnel is headed east."

"That's taking us the opposite way," Doc observed.

"It doesn't matter," Jax interjected, her tone indicating a deeper connection with the route.

"How can you be so sure, Jax?" Cal asked, a hint of scepticism in his voice.

"I don't know ... call it intuition," she admitted, struggling to articulate her certainty.

"We should trust her instincts. They've led us right so far. I know it's against logic, but that seems to work when we're with her," Doc explained to a hesitant Cal.

Though unconvinced, Cal reluctantly agreed to follow Jax's lead into the eastward tunnel.

Meanwhile, Maddox was also consulting his GPS. "7.8232, 126.1749. We're about ten kilometres east of the target."

"So, we need to head west," Bato inferred.

Standing at a T-junction in the track, Maddox pointed the device to his left. "That way's east."

"But we need to go west," Digger interjected, feeling an innate pull in that direction, especially towards Jax and Doc. Maddox nodded in agreement and led them on a descending path toward the valley floor.

After trekking for about a kilometre inside the mountain, Cal finally saw light at the end of the tunnel. The passage opened onto a trail that descended from the heart of the mountain to the verdant valley below. Cal paused at the threshold, mesmerized by the panorama, and waited for the others to catch up. Jax soon stood beside him, sharing in the wonder. "How beautiful."

"Yes, a hidden valley," Cal responded, his voice reflecting a sense of awe.

The rest of the group joined them, each person pausing to take in the sight of the untouched landscape.

"It looks pristine," Doc observed, scanning the valley.

Cal pulled out a pair of binoculars from his kitbag and began surveying the terrain. He murmured in disbelief, "Well, I'll be..."

"What is it?" Jax asked, her curiosity piqued.

"Not so pristine, there are ruins down there ... they look like Mayan structures you'd find in the Yucatan." Cal adjusted the binoculars, focusing on the mountainside. "Wait!" He handed the binoculars to Doc. "Have a look at this."

Doc took the binoculars, his gaze following Cal's direction. His eyes narrowed as he spotted movement. "People," he whispered.

"Let me see," Jax said, reaching for the binoculars.

Doc passed them to her. She focused on the figures making their way down the mountainside. "That's Digger, I thought so. They're descending into the valley," she said, lowering the binoculars. Her eyes met Cal's. "He's leading them right to us."

Cal's lips curled into a smirk as he took back the binoculars for another look. "I can see Maddox ... along with three others, Digger, probably Juno Santos, and one of Maddox's men—looks like he's got an eye bandaged." His voice was tinged with anticipation. He glanced at Dino and Vehnee, ready to spring into action. "Right, here's the plan..."

CHAPTER TWELVE

Cal had his team strategically positioned where the track Maddox was on would meet the valley floor. The rocky terrain provided ample cover. Jax and Doc were stationed behind a large boulder, a short distance from the ambush site, with a clear view of the impending action. They waited in silence.

Soon, Maddox emerged into the clearing and paused, allowing Bato, Digger, and Juno to catch up. Cal had planned meticulously; aware that Maddox might use either Digger or Juno as a shield, he had positioned Dino and Vehnee to quickly isolate them at the right moment. Everyone held their breath, waiting for Cal's signal.

Jax and Doc watched anxiously, hoping the operation would unfold without casualties.

In a swift move, Cal stepped out from his hiding spot directly into Maddox's path, gun aimed and ready. Simultaneously, Dino moved to secure Digger and Juno, while Vehnee confronted Bato, pressing a gun into his back. It was a perfectly executed manoeuvre. Maddox, caught off-guard, didn't even have a chance to draw his weapon. The chorus of 'hands up' from Cal and Vehnee had Maddox and Bato reaching skyward in surrender.

As Jax and Doc emerged, Digger rushed to embrace his sister, while Doc and Juno exchanged firm handshakes.

Just when Dino was about to handcuff Bato, the situation took a sudden turn. Bato, with a swift motion, drew a knife and swiftly manoeuvred behind Dino, pressing the blade to his throat. Everyone froze, the tension palpable.

"Wanna lose him, Christo?" Maddox taunted, smirking confidently.

Thunk! The standoff was abruptly interrupted by an arrow, adorned with brightly coloured feathers, thudding into a tree trunk beside Bato's head. Startled, Bato hesitated, realising the next arrow might not miss. Seizing the moment of distraction, Dino skilfully disarmed and handcuffed Bato. Cal then subdued and cuffed Maddox.

"Sit down," Cal commanded. "Dino, bring them here." He positioned Maddox and Bato back to back, with Vehnee standing guard, while he and Dino scouted the jungle for the unseen archer. After a thorough but fruitless search, they returned.

"See anything?" Doc inquired.

"Nothing, but there's a track leading through the ruins into the jungle. It heads towards our GPS coordinates. Our destination seems to be on the other side of the valley," Cal reported, his voice steady but alert.

A little while later, acutely aware of unseen eyes watching them from the jungle, the group set off in single file, with Cal leading the way along the track they had discovered. The thought of being at the mercy of an elusive archer, capable of striking at any moment, cast an eerie feeling over the group. While the others were apprehensive about the hidden threat, Doc's attention was drawn to the ruins overgrown with vegetation flanking the track. He busied himself photographing them as they walked.

"They look ancient," Digger remarked, peering at the crumbling structures.

"At least five hundred years old," Doc responded, snapping pictures. "These ruins were likely toppled by earthquakes. This is a volcanic area, after all. I'd say this valley could be a fault line running between what were once active volcanoes. Considering what we found inside the mountain, there's probably still volcanic activity here."

Doc's casual observation introduced a new layer of anxiety among the group, but as usual, he seemed unfazed by it.

"Wonder who that archer is?" Jax mused out loud.

"It might be the indigenous people," Juno suggested. "The Subanon are known for their use of bright colours, like the quill on that arrow."

"Are they dangerous?" Jax inquired, a hint of concern in her voice.

"I don't think so," Juno replied. "The arrow was probably just a warning, maybe to keep us away from their hunting grounds."

Carter was sitting in his office when the phone rang. "Yes, who? Oh, right, put her through. Hello, Dr Jimenez, how can I help you?"

"We've got them," came the voice on the other end.

Carter rose slowly, a wave of excitement overwhelming him. He stammered, "I, I ... Which ones?"

Just then, Janet burst into the office, her expression tense with anticipation. Knowing the call was from the Philippines, she hoped it was news about Jax. It had been two months since the expedition had vanished. Carter gestured to her, indicating it was indeed news.

"Only three," Dr Jimenez reported. "Juno Santos, Vincent Lee, and Jax De Loite."

Carter sank back into his chair, relief washing over him. With emotion thick in his voice, he asked, "Is Jax alright?"

"Yes, she'll need a few days in the hospital..."

He cut in anxiously, "And Doc? Santos?"

Janet, unable to contain her eagerness, mouthed, "Jax?"

Carter nodded, confirming her hopes.

Overjoyed, Janet quickly left the office to spread the news.

"Both men have injuries, but they'll recover," Dr Jimenez continued.

"And Cal? Anything about him?" Carter inquired, grasping for more information.

"We're hoping Jax can fill in the details once she's well enough," came the reply.

Just then, Janet returned with Tilly, who was in tears, clearly moved by the news.

"I'll be arranging for my team to fly out tonight," Carter declared, ready to take action.

The next afternoon, Janet, Tilly, and a two-man film crew arrived at Davao airport and were greeted by a driver holding a 'NewsLine' sign. After checking into a hotel, they were driven to San Pedro Hospital.

Dr Christina Jimenez met them in the lobby. As they walked to Jax's room, Janet inquired, "How is she?"

"She's much better now; she might be discharged tomorrow," Christina replied.

"And Doc?"

"Likely, they'll all leave tomorrow."

Outside Jax's room, a nurse conversed with Dr Jimenez in Cebuano. After a brief exchange, Christina relayed, "Only two visitors for now."

Tilly, fluent in Cebuano, asked about Jax's condition. Receiving an affirmative response, she and Janet were allowed to enter Jax's room.

Inside, they found Jax sitting up in bed, looking out of place in the hospital setting. Tilly rushed to embrace her, while Janet sat beside her, holding her hand.

"Are you alright, darling? We've been so worried..." Tilly said, tears in her eyes.

"I can imagine," Jax replied with a reassuring smile, squeezing Janet's hand. "I didn't expect you to come, Janet."

"Hey, this is a Next Files story. We even have a camera crew waiting outside," Janet said with a smile.

"They told me I might be discharged tomorrow. Let's do the interview at the Davao Museum, while it's still all fresh in my mind," Jax suggested, her voice still weak. "And check on Doc and Juno. Doc's been documenting everything."

A nurse entered, speaking briefly with Tilly in Cebuano. Tilly nodded, then turned to Janet. "The doctor's coming soon; we have to leave. They'll let us know if Jax can be discharged in the morning."

Janet stood up, leaned over, and gave Jax a gentle kiss on the cheek. "We'll set everything up. Get some rest now."

Unable to visit Doc and Juno due to their ongoing consultation with the doctor, Janet and Tilly decided to head back to the hotel to prepare for the upcoming interview.

The next morning, Janet received an update from Dr Jimenez. Jax was to be discharged at 10 am and would be taken directly to the Museum. Doc and Juno's discharge, however, would be delayed until early afternoon due to the doctor's surgery schedule. So, the plan was set: Janet and her team would head to the Museum, while Tilly would visit the Santos family in Tula.

An hour before Jax's arrival at the museum, Janet, cameraman Rod, and sound engineer Steve were escorted to the boardroom by the receptionist. Shortly after, Dr Jimenez joined them, and Janet inquired if they could use a more visually engaging setting for the interview, like the exhibition hall.

With the museum closed to the public on Mondays, they had the liberty to choose their backdrop. They settled on a striking diorama: a primitive, indigenous hunter poised with a bow and arrow, targeting a massive crocodile. Behind him stood a woman, balancing a wicker basket of yams and cradling a baby, with an erupting volcano looming in the background. The dramatic scene, both intriguing and intimidating, seemed fitting for the tone of the interview.

As the crew set up chairs and lighting in front of the exhibit, Janet mused over the choice. "Absolutely, it's perfect. Sensationalizing is a key component of our show."

Christina raised an eyebrow. "This scene represents the Homo Luzonensis, the oldest known hominin found in the Philippines, dating back sixty-seven thousand years."

Janet chuckled, "We're not exactly historical documentarians, Doctor. We're more like a real-life version of the X-Files, remember that show from the 90s?"

"I was quite the Fox Mulder fan," Christina admitted with a smile.

"Our job is to create 48 minutes of riveting TV that keeps viewers and advertisers hooked. It's all about ratings for us."

"So, never let the truth get in the way of a good story?" Christina asked, half-jokingly.

Janet responded, "It's not quite like that. Jax, following in her father's footsteps, is a stickler for facts, and Doc, he insists on accuracy."

Christina's phone chimed. "That's my cue to collect Jax. I'll be back in fifteen minutes. Feel free to help yourselves to coffee and snacks from the canteen."

Fifteen minutes later, as promised, Christina returned with Jax. Janet greeted her with noticeable relief. "You look much better today. Feeling up to this?"

"I'm good, just really dehydrated," Jax replied, eyeing the primitive hunter scene behind her. "A figure like that might have saved us out there."

"I'm so curious to hear about everything," Janet responded. "Do you need to script anything first?"

"No, I think it's best if I just tell it as it happened," Jax decided.

"Okay, we'll capture it raw and edit as needed. Are you okay with this background?"

"Yeah, it's intriguing. Did anyone talk to Doc?" Jax inquired, a hint of concern in her voice.

"Not yet," Janet replied.

Christina, catching the cue, interjected. "I spoke to him. You want to know about his phone, right?"

Janet's face lit up with excitement at the prospect of the documentary evidence.

Relief washed over Janet and Jax. The possibility of having a comprehensive photo account from Doc added immeasurable value to their story.

After Jax was prepped with makeup and a change of clothes, she took her seat against the backdrop of Homo Luzonensis. Janet positioned herself off-camera. Rod, the cameraman, had his equipment poised, and Steve was fine-tuning the audio setup. The atmosphere was charged with anticipation as they prepared to roll.

CHAPTER
THIRTEEN

Transcript of interview with Jax de Loite:
"A wise man once told me, 'it can take a lifetime for you to arrive at where you began,' and that's how these last two months feel to me now. That man Dr Henry de Loite, a renowned archaeologist and award-winning journalist. More importantly, he was my dad. Like what happened to my mother in 2003, he vanished on an expedition into the jungles of Mindanao in 2017. So here I am, back where my colleagues and I started our search for him.

We had specific GPS coordinates from my father's diary, discovered after he went missing. Our team for the jungle expedition consisted of myself from The Next Files, my colleague Doc Lee, my brother Digger de Loite, Juno Santos (the son of my father's Filipino guide who also disappeared), and a security detail of three experienced mercenaries led by Cal Christo.

There was another team led by a man we'll just call Maddox, a notorious dealer in black-market antiquities. Maddox believed my father had found a lost city of Aztecs, complete with treasure that could make him rich.

You might be asking yourself, "Aztecs in the Philippines?" Yes, indeed. My parents devoted years to researching the theory that after the fall of the Aztec Empire in 1520, the Spanish established a port in Acapulco. From there, galleons would sail to the Philippines, discovered by Magellan in 1521. By 1530, the first of these ships set sail for the Philippines, carrying, among their crews, Aztec slaves—some from royal lineages.

Upon landing in Mindanao, these expeditions were in dire straits—starving and desperate for fresh resources. The Aztec slaves were sent to gather supplies, but they never returned. Finding the dense jungles of Mindanao reminiscent of their native Central America, they fled, seizing the opportunity to start a new life.

My parents discovered evidence suggesting that the descendants of these Aztec slaves were still thriving in the remote Diwata Mountains of Mindanao. During an expedition in 2003, my father had an unbelievable experience—he saw my mother being abducted by what appeared to be a birdman, dressed in the regalia of an Aztec shaman. She was never seen again, and this event consumed my father. He was convinced she had been taken by descendants of the Aztecs, determined to conceal their existence from the world. In 2017, my father and Ito Santos ventured back into the jungle, but they too disappeared. All we had to go on was my father's diary, found near Ito's remains.

Years later, armed with this diary and driven by a need to unravel the mystery, I organised an expedition to trace my father's last journey.

Before we even really kicked off our expedition, we hit a major snag. Maddox, who was racing us to the same coordinates, snatched my brother Digger and Juno Santos. He wanted to use them as leverage, thinking if we found any treasure first, he could bargain with them.

Maddox took a different path to those coordinates, which ended up being a bad shout for his team; he lost one of his guys. Turns out, with a bit of help from Digger, Maddox got more than he bargained for—he found us. So there we were, in the depths of the jungle, with Maddox and his sidekick Bato as our captives.

This valley we stumbled into was like something out of an adventure movie—all these giant, toppled ruins that looked like they could be from Aztec or Mayan times. And the creepiest part? It felt like we were being watched the whole time. Hidden eyes in the bushes, you know? We found a path cutting through the valley, which was maybe half a kilometre across. We were about halfway through when, out of nowhere, Cal gets hit with a blow dart in the neck. The guy's a mountain, six foot six of pure muscle, and this dart just took him down. Doc examined the dart and said it looked like the kind they use in Central America for stunning animals. Great, now we had to lug Cal's unconscious bulk across the rest of the valley.

By the time we made it to the other side, the sun was setting, and we were all on edge, expecting another sneak attack any second. We crashed in a clearing, totally wiped out.

Worried about another attack this time from the cover of darkness, I asked advice from Cal's men, Vehnee and Dino how to defend ourselves. They were clueless.

"That don't know … they only take orders … You'll need more than them to defend the camp tonight," Maddox said gruffly, motioning with his bound hands, clearly wanting to be freed.

"We can't trust you, not after what you've pulled," Doc retorted sharply.

"Yeah, good shout, I can dig that. But let's face reality—there could be a whole group of them out there. You need my experience," Maddox argued, his fear evident.

"You're just freaked out because you won't be able to defend yourself bound up like a pig," Juno snarled. He had no time for Maddox.

"Maddox is right," Digger said. "Look, we're all in the same boat. We don't have to trust Maddox, but with Cal down, he'll be of more value than we would being tied up."

Vehnee and Dino remained silent, but the rest of us, even Juno, realised Digger had a point.

Digger cut them loose. We quickly prepared a campfire, and Maddox organized sentries, assigning four-hour shifts to keep watch through the night.

It was super late, like 3 am, when I suddenly woke up. The campfire had died down, and Bato, who was supposed to be on watch, was out cold. That's when I heard something rustling in the shadows.

Peering into the tangle of vines, I could just make out a figure staring back at me. It was like a birdman, except it had a snake for a head. Creepy, right? But weirdly, I wasn't scared, just really curious about whether he was cool or trouble.

Then I heard another noise and spotted a second figure, clearly a girl from the look of it. I decided to go for it and got out of my sleeping bag, slowly walking towards her. They just stood there, not moving an inch. I stretched out my hand, you know, trying to be friendly.

Up close, she was striking, all painted up with intricate patterns and decked out in colourful feathers. Her eyes, dark and intense, suddenly flicked to my right. I turned and saw Digger had joined me.

Then Digger did something weird—he put on our dad's old hat. No idea why, it just seemed like the thing to do at the moment. As soon as he did, both these mysterious people dropped to their knees, like we were someone important. Digger and I just looked at each other, totally confused.

"It's the hat," I whispered to him. "Try going closer."

So, Digger crept over to them. They stayed there, almost bowing and making this low, chanting sound. When he gently touched the snake-guy's shoulder, the dude just flopped right onto the ground. Digger helped him back up, reassuring him we weren't there to cause trouble.

Then the guy inside the snake mask spoke, his voice muffled but definitely in English, "You, spirit."

We were totally freaked when the birdman with a snake head seemed to recognize Digger as Henry, his step-dad. They must have known him! But then, out of nowhere, a gunshot split the air. Those two mysterious figures just bolted into the jungle like ghosts. It turned out Bato had woken up, seen them, and fired a warning shot. The whole camp was up in a flash, all freaked out. It took us a bit to explain that we thought it was actually a friendly visit.

For the rest of the night, none of us got much sleep. Digger, Doc, Juno, and I were up late, trying to make sense of why the visitors reacted the way they did. But one thing was clear—the birdman had recognised something of Henry in Digger.

The next morning, we were all around the campfire, nursing cups of tea and rehashing last night's craziness. That's when Maddox piped up, "I reckon that was a sign. They knew Henry. We should find their place."

Juno shot back, "You're just after treasure."

Maddox was like, "So what? We've all got our reasons."

Right then, we heard Cal groan. He was finally waking up. After shaking off his grogginess, we decided to check out more ruins around the valley.

We stumbled upon this epic ruin, still pretty much intact. Doc was all over it, taking pics of the carvings on the stones. Meanwhile, Digger and I were drawn to what appeared to be a well. Digger noticed fresh footprints around it and guessed, "Bet our friends from last night popped out of here."

Finding a colourful feather on the ground, I agreed. "Looks like it." I mused, "What if this well leads to their secret city?"

Digger was like, "And what if they don't wanna be found?"

Maddox, always the type to push limits, said with a challenging tone, "Too bad for them." There he was, typical Maddox, gun in hand, pointing it at us.

"Dude, chill out," Digger tried to reason with him. But in a twist straight out of nowhere, Maddox suddenly clutched his neck as if stung by a wasp and crumpled to the ground, out cold.

Then, like a scene from a wild adventure movie, a group of birdmen emerged from the jungle, encircling us. They were followed by more birdmen escorting the rest of our crew. The snake-headed guy from last night, who was surprisingly muscular, stepped up, bowed to Digger and me, and then gestured towards the well.

Bato, panicking, shouted, "They're gonna sacrifice us or something!" But mid-scream, a dart hit him in the throat, and he dropped just like Maddox. Thankfully, Cal and the rest of the guys kept their cool and didn't draw their guns. The girl from last night, adorned in her stunning plumage, stepped forward from the ranks of birdmen. After bowing respectfully to Digger and me, she reached out and gently took my hand, leading me towards the well. I've got to admit, I was pretty nervous. My mind raced with images from those documentaries I'd seen on the History Channel about ancient remains discovered at the bottom of wells in Yucatan and Mexico, often linked to human sacrifices. Was I about to face the same fate?

CHAPTER FOURTEEN

Glancing at Doc, I could see he was apprehensive. As I was led past Digger, our eyes met, and he nodded reassuringly, sharing my sense that these people weren't a threat. The girl with the plumage stopped me right at the edge of the well. Looking down, it was dark and somewhat menacing. The snake-headed guy gestured, and a younger man with a coiled, knotted rope over his shoulder approached us. He quickly secured the rope to a large rock with a hole carved in it specifically for this purpose. My fears of being thrown in were quelled. The girl descended first, climbing into the well and holding the rope, then reached up for my hand. I followed her lead.

Descending the ten metres was surprisingly easy, thanks to the knots. Climbing up, though, would definitely be tougher. The cool air was a relief as we went lower. When I reached the bottom, I saw Digger making his way down.

Eventually, everyone got down, and the last person closed a seal partway down, cutting off the light. Then, out of the darkness, torches were lit by several of the natives.

"Where's Maddox and Bato?" I asked Doc.

"They left them up top. Seems they figured out those two were trouble," he replied.

"I hope they'll be okay," I said, somewhat concerned.

"Maddox can handle himself," Doc assured me.

Soon, we were being ushered single file along a narrow tunnel. It felt like we were in another one of those ancient volcanic vents Doc had mentioned. Our footsteps echoed as we trudged along the damp floor. After about twenty minutes, we entered a larger cavern, adorned with stalactites and featuring a hot spring. Stopping for a break, we splashed our faces with the tepid mineral water.

"This would be perfect to soak in," I said, half-joking.

"If this is like the springs near my village, it's full of healthy minerals," Juno commented.

"Juno, can you figure out what language they speak?" Doc inquired.

Juno tried speaking to the girl asking her name, first in Cebuano, then in Chabacano, the language of southern Mindanao. She responded with a smile and said in English, "My name Atzi," then pointed at me.

"I'm Jax, and these are Digger, Doc, and Juno," I introduced us.

Atzi smiled warmly again, then gestured towards Digger and me, "You, brother and sister, you, children of Henry."

We were completely mind-blown. Before we could delve deeper, the leader signalled for us to follow him into another tunnel.

Winding through the labyrinth, we finally emerged into an enormous cavern. It was massive, the biggest I'd ever seen. We looked down from the precipice to see an incredible sight two hundred metres below us—an unmistakably Aztec city.

As we stood marvelling at the sight before us, a massive cavern bathed in light streaming through cracks in its domed ceiling, the ground suddenly began to shake. The snake-headed man, balancing himself, raised his staff high like some sort of epic hero and yelled over the roar, "Quetzalcoatl, we hear you!"

Doc leaned in and whispered to me, "Quetzalcoatl was like the top god for the Aztecs."

The earthquake was brief but intense, rattling everything around us. Dust swirled in the shafts of light, casting a strange, eerie glow over the whole scene. I noticed more fissures had appeared in the ceiling, letting in even more light.

Turning to Atzi, I said, "Earthquake."

She looked seriously worried. "The gods are angry more and more."

Doc gave me a look. "If we get a bigger quake, this place is toast."

Just then, Cal joined us. "Our friend with the snake head speaks reasonable English, believe it or not. He's saying these quakes are getting more frequent. If a big one hits, this whole place could collapse."

I felt a surge of urgency. "We have to do something. These people think it's angry gods causing this. If the roof caves in…"

Doc's face was grim. "It's not 'if', Jax. It's 'when'."

Navigating down the path that zigzagged along the cliff took us another hour. The cliff-face itself looked fragile, as if one strong shake could trigger a landslide. Reaching the bottom, we were met with wide-eyed stares and pointing fingers from the villagers. Their excitement was palpable; to them, we must have seemed like gods. The village houses were made of white stucco, which Doc identified as clay. At the heart of the village, laid out in neat squares, stood a thirty-metre-tall step pyramid, strikingly similar to the Pyramid of Kukulkan in Yucatan. Next to it was a grand building, looking every bit a palace. Our group was ushered inside, with Atzi continuing to hold my hand, guiding me along.

Inside, we walked on a narrow crimson carpet leading to a throne set upon a dais. As we approached, I looked up and my breath caught in my throat. Seated on the throne was a withered corpse clutching a golden staff. In a moment of shock, I realised— the corpse was my father, Henry de Loite.

The days following the shocking discovery of our mummified father were filled with eye-opening revelations. Our snake-headed leader, Ocelot, revealed himself without his mask. Astonishingly, he was named after the original slave, a grandson of Moctezuma, who led the escape from the Spanish galleon in 1530. Ocelot was the same age as me, and to our amazement, we learned that he was named by my dad. It was like a story coming to life, one my father had shared with me in my childhood.

Coatl, the elder shaman who was well into his seventies, recounted my dad's story. After being found by the well, my father was brought to this hidden city. His companion, Ito, had fled in fear.

Digger and I found ourselves standing in a crypt, a place that felt both eerie and sacred. At the centre of this ancient chamber was a sarcophagus, the focal point of the room. What took our breath away was the carving on it—it bore an unmistakable likeness to our mother, Cindy.

The truth unravelled like a long-held secret finally coming to light. Our mother, after her abduction, hadn't just survived; she had become a figure of reverence, ascending to the status of an Aztec Queen among the descendants of the Aztec slaves. And our father, in his relentless pursuit to find her, eventually found his way to this hidden civilization. Rather than returning, he joined her, becoming their King.

Together, they ruled this secluded society for three years. Their reign, as Doc suggested, probably ended due to malaria.

The idea that our parents had chosen to leave the 21st Century to rule as the king and queen of an Aztec society was mind-boggling to Digger and me. But the biggest shock was yet to come.

After we were all comfortably settled into rooms in the palace, each of us faced different choices about what to do next. Cal and his men were eager to head back to Davao, now that their mission was completed. Doc, Digger, and I, however, were captivated by the opportunity to learn more about these remarkable people and their unique history. Juno seemed content but I had a feeling he might opt to leave with Cal if given the chance.

Doc was thoroughly immersed in his work, documenting every aspect he could. He discovered that the city was called Tepanec, translating to 'people of the valley' in Nahuatl. The city was a bustling community of about three-thousand people, complete with market gardens, aqua-culture and chicken farms. They cultivated crops familiar to their Aztec heritage, like corn, chilies, xocoatl (chocolate), and cafenyolli (coffee beans). It was as though they had recreated a slice of Anahuac, the pre-colonial name for what is now Mexico, in this secluded part of the Philippines.

Life in Tepanec seemed almost idyllic, although we learned that they still worshipped the feathered serpent god Quetzalcoatl. Thankfully, my parents had guided their beliefs and practices wisely, avoiding the pitfalls of modern society. My father had always had a commanding presence, which I recalled was part of the reason Digger had left home.

But then came the most unexpected proposition. Ocelot and Coatl suggested that Digger and I assume the roles of King and

Queen of Tepanec. We tried to explain the impracticality of this, given that we were siblings, but they insisted, citing royal family traditions of interbreeding. They even presented us with a hand-written book of Tepanec laws, authored in English by our father, to reinforce their point. Digger and I requested time to discuss their proposal, and they agreed to give us until sunrise. That evening, our group gathered to debate this extraordinary offer.

Digger was the first to speak up, his tone grave. "I don't think it's an offer, it's a demand," he said.

I had to agree. "They wouldn't have given a deadline if it was an offer," I pointed out.

Doc, deep in thought, finally chimed in. "So if it's a demand, if you don't comply what's going to happen?"

Digger and I shared a look, realising the gravity of the situation. "We didn't ask," I admitted.

Cal's voice broke the tense silence. "I don't like it. Look, it's all a bit quixotic here, and far too amiable for my liking. These people are warriors, they've survived for centuries undetected, until your parents came along. It doesn't seem as rulers they changed their ways. I have a gut feeling there's something being hidden from us, and I think it's their real way of life."

Dino nodded in agreement. "I've got to say the shaman Coatl gives me the creeps," he confessed.

Doc had been pacing, his mind racing. He stopped and turned to us. "I think you're right Cal, you too Dino. Documenting the place, I've been prevented access to certain areas ... for one, inside the pyramid ... and like I don't mean just being told not to enter, some places are heavily guarded."

Juno's question redirected our attention. "Anything in the book of laws written by your father, Jax?"

I sighed, recalling the contents. "To be honest," I explained, "it had nothing good to say other than some basic ten commandment-like laws. The punishments listed for crimes are reminiscent of the barbaric rituals described by de Tapia in the 16th Century conquest of the Aztec Empire."

"Maybe that's what they're hiding?" Cal proposed.

We realised that before making any decision, Digger and I needed more clarity on what was at stake. We agreed to seek answers and adjourned the meeting until we had a better understanding.

Digger and I agreed it would be best to avoid Coatl and instead bring our questions to Ocelot, who seemed more approachable. As we stepped out of the palace and into the market square, we noticed a crowd of villagers gathering, their expressions a mix of anticipation and solemnity. Among them was Atzi. Our eyes met, and she walked over to us.

"What's going on, Atzi? They look pretty excited," I asked, noting the unusual buzz in the air.

"There will be a sacrifice to the gods at dawn," she replied with a sense of gravity.

Digger, taken aback, asked, "What will be sacrificed?"

"Outlaws," she said simply.

My mind focused on more pressing matters, I inquired, "Can you take us to Ocelot? We need to talk to him."

"I take you," Atzi agreed.

She led us through the now-emptying market square, past two guards, to the back of the pyramid a part we hadn't seen before. She ushered us into an empty room within the pyramid, asked us to wait, and disappeared through another door. When she returned, it wasn't with Ocelot but with Coatl, who seemed less than pleased to see us.

Digger, trying to ease the tension, started, "Sorry to disturb you, Coatl, but we have some important questions…"

"Yes?" Coatl prompted, his tone terse.

I jumped straight in, "If we decline to rule, will we be free to leave?"

"It was not a request," Coatl responded bluntly.

"Please, just answer the question," I pressed.

"Only the gods can decide," he said, his voice filled with reverence.

We were left unsatisfied with his response, but it was clear that was all he would offer. Digger then asked, "And how is that decided?"

Coatl replied dismissively, "You have the Book of Laws, you can see for yourself. Now, I must attend to other matters." He turned and walked away, his footsteps echoing in the room.

"I take you back," Atzi offered quietly.

Upon our return to the palace, Atzi looked at me with a hint of hope, "If you leave, can I come?"

I held her hand, meeting her gaze. "We'll see," I replied, knowing the answer was far from what she wanted to hear. She nodded, a universal sign of understanding mixed with disappointment, and walked away.

"I don't think she's very happy," Digger noted.

"No, and neither am I," I admitted. "What Coatl said is not what I wanted to hear."

CHAPTER FIFTEEN

Before telling the others, we checked the Book of Laws and found something about our situation: 'denial of an edict'. "It says it is punishable by death," I said.

"That's a bit extreme, isn't it?" Digger stressed.

"Actually, most things that go against an official order end with the death penalty."

"I thought our folks were pacifists," Digger said.

"So did I. Maybe they got a bit power-crazy?"

"What if they wrote this when they were sick? Like, if they had malaria, they might've been off their heads."

"That's a solid point. And how were they treating it?"

"We should ask Ocelot."

"No," I said, "I think Coatl's got him wrapped around his finger. We'll ask Atzi."

"Smart thinking. But first, let's update the crew."

We gathered everyone and spilled the beans. Cal was all worried about this dawn sacrifice thing, thinking it might be important for us.

"There's no doubt about it, we've got to get out of here quick," Cal said, pretty intense.

"These pagans are basically the devil..." Vehnee started, going all religious on us.

I cut him off, "Let's not get into that, mate ... Right, the plan."

"Your bond with Atzi might be our ace. She seems like she's searching for a way out too," Cal suggested.

He was spot on. Atzi was our key. We planned to meet up just before dawn to see the sacrifice. Digger thought Dad wrote the laws in words the villagers would get, like 'sacrifice', but more as a metaphor. I really hoped he was right.

I barely slept that night, too much on my mind. We got up early, before the sun, and headed to the market square. Strangely, it was empty. We kept going and saw people heading to the pyramid's front door. Looked like a gathering, so we joined in line.

Surprisingly, the guards just let us through. Inside was this huge hall, the ceiling reaching up to the apex of the pyramid. Loads of people were already sitting down. We found a spot and stood against a side wall. Ocelot was standing alone on a platform at the end, in his colourful outfit and snake mask. The hall was super quiet, even with so many people.

I noticed Atzi nearby. She got up and joined us.

The amount of gold in the room caught my eye, from the candle holders to Ocelot's gear and the gold staff he held.

"If Maddox could see all this gold, his eyes would be bugging out," I whispered to Doc.

The crowd started murmuring, and Doc whispered back, "Speak of the devil."

Two guards came from the back of the platform, and there was Maddox, in chains.

"So when Atzi here told me 'outlaws' were to be sacrificed..." I began.

"They'd caught Maddox and Bato," Doc chimed in.

Right then, Bato showed up behind Maddox, also in chains and flanked by guards.

I nearly jumped out of my skin when this loud blast from conch shell trumpets echoed through the place. We all turned to the entrance. This guy, probably Coatl, walked in, decked out in this crazy bird feather gown and an insane headdress, topped with a freaky skull mask. As he moved down the aisle between the sitting crowd towards the dais, he was followed by a bunch of musicians. They played clay flutes, ocarinas, rattles, and drums. The music sounded pretty cheerful, totally not matching our vibes.

When Coatl got to the dais, the music stopped dead. The musicians found spots on either side of the dais, while Coatl climbed the stairs to join Ocelot.

Coatl faced everyone and started shouting in Nahuatl. I nudged Atzi for a translation.

"He is speaking for the gods; they are mad. An offering must be made to them. It will be the outlaws."

I gulped when Ocelot pulled a dagger from his staff and handed it to Coatl, who lifted it with both hands above his head like he was offering it to the gods. That's when I realised this wasn't going to be symbolic; it was legit.

I asked Atzi quickly, "Did you ever meet my dad?"

"Yes, but he was sick, your mum already with the gods. Your dad taught me English."

"Who looked after him when he was ill?"

"Coatl, he is the medicine man."

"What did he give him?"

"Angel's trumpet."

Doc, who overheard, said, "Angel's trumpet is psilocybin; that's a serious hallucinogen."

"Magic mushrooms, no wonder," I muttered. Now it made sense why my dad wrote such weird stuff in the Book of Laws; he was off his face.

Coatl signalled, and the guards brought Maddox and Bato up the stairs to the dais.

I glared at Cal, "We've got to stop this."

As Coatl held the blade, Maddox freaked out and shouted, "You've got the wrong person! I was ordered by Jax de Loite to shoot your warriors!"

The crowd stirred, a murmur of anger spreading, and a sea of eyes turned to stare at me.

"That's a lie!" I fired back, loud and clear.

Without missing a beat, Cal sprang into action, charging down the aisle towards the dais like a marauding bull. Reaching the stairs, two guards blocked him with crossed spears. But Cal wasn't having any of it; he ripped the spears apart, dashed up the stairs, and snatched the knife right out of Coatl's frail grip. Vehnee and Dino weren't far behind, holding their ground at the stair's base, ready for a scrap.

Cal grabbed Coatl, yanked off his mask, pressed the blade to his throat, and bellowed, "Order them to let the prisoners go, or you'll be the one to be sacrificed!"

Just then, Ocelot lunged at Cal with his golden staff, knocking the blade out of his hand.

But Cal, towering over Ocelot, grabbed the staff, swung it hard across Ocelot's chest, and sent him flying off the dais. Cal scooped up the blade and flung it to Dino, who caught it mid-air and stood over Ocelot, making sure he stayed down.

Cal, holding the staff high, threatened Coatl, "Tell your warriors to back off!"

By now, the dais was ringed by twenty spear-wielding warriors. Coatl, realising he was cornered, gave in and ordered the guards to stand down. The immediate threat was over, but Maddox's betrayal hadn't escaped my notice.

We were all watching intently. As soon as Maddox and Bato were freed from their ropes by the guards, Maddox grabbed the golden staff Cal had set down, and both he and Bato bolted out of there. Nobody tried to stop them.

"That guy just can't help himself," I muttered to no-one in particular. Then I heard this soft whimpering next to me. "What's wrong, Atzi?"

"Now there will be no choice; a sacrifice must be made to the gods. Without the prisoners, it will be a virgin, and I have been chosen."

"No, no, no, Atzi, that's just not happening," I tried to assure her.

"You can only stop it as Queen."

It hit me like a ton of bricks what I had to do. Without a second thought, I yelled, "Coatl, I accept! I will be your Queen!"

Digger gave me this look like I'd lost my marbles. "You've got to be kidding."

Back in the palace, we called another meeting. I had to lay out my plan. It made sense to everyone. We'd bail from Tepanec right after I got crowned.

Atzi showed up with a message from Coatl; they were going to crown me Queen at the next sunset, Aztec-style. That was the good part. The bad news? To honour my rise and please the gods, they planned to sacrifice Atzi at dawn. Great, now we had a deadline: to get out of Tepanec with Atzi before the sun came up. Lucky for us, Atzi, being fluent in English, had been appointed as my lady-in-waiting.

The crowning ceremony was like something out of a movie. After Atzi and some other handmaidens decked me out, I stepped out of the palace, all dressed up, on my way to the pyramid. Doc and the others were waiting; Doc even shot a video. Digger was all dressed up too, ready to play his part as my brother giving the bride away—to the gods, no less. I was draped in so much colourful bird plumage I felt like a turkey. The head-dress, loaded with beads, feathers, and gold wire, was so heavy I could barely keep my head up. My hair was woven with gold, and my hands and feet sparkled with gold dust.

"You look amazing ... a true Queen," Digger whispered, escorting me past the guys.

Entering the pyramid was surreal; the whole place was packed. There was a golden throne on the dais, with Ocelot and Coatl standing by in their ceremonial gear.

The band was bigger this time, playing a tune that this time seemed perfect for the moment.

Digger led me up to the dais, Atzi holding my dress train. It felt like I was in some weird wedding, but the idea of marrying gods? Nope, that's where I drew the line.

Coatl, now wearing a golden death mask of my dad instead of the skull mask, which honestly freaked me out, took my hand from Digger and led me to the throne.

Everything went silent as Coatl switched to English for my benefit. "We are privileged the gods sent us the daughter of King Henry and Queen Cindy to ascend the absent throne of Tepanec."

Then he did something wild. He cut his palm with a ceremonial blade, held his fist over my head, and let his blood drip onto my face. The crowd roared their approval while I struggled not to lose my lunch. Once my face was stained red, Coatl stopped, the conch shells blasted, and just like that, I was crowned.

Coatl announced, "As the sun sets, a new sun will rise as Queen Jax!"

The place erupted in cheers, but 'Queen Jax'? That just didn't sound right to me.

CHAPTER
SIXTEEN

Ocelot had sent a squad of warriors after Maddox and Bato to get back the golden staff. We doubted they'd end up captured this time. The celebration stretched into the night, which was a bit awkward for us since we were itching to make our getaway. The drink they served, Pulque, was like beer but made from fermented Agave sap, and man, did it pack a punch. By 3 am, the party had pretty much fizzled out, with everyone but our group sleeping it off. We thought sneaking out would be a breeze, but just as we were about to make our move, the ground started shaking—and it this time it was major quake.

Slipping out of the palace under the veil of night, with the ground still trembling beneath us, Doc suddenly looked up at the cavern ceiling and said urgently, "It's going to collapse, look!" We all craned our necks to see.

Fissures had widened, and massive chunks of the roof were tumbling down, threatening to smash into the city. We bolted, running as fast as we could.

Finally reaching the bottom of the well, we let out a collective sigh of relief. The rope left by the warriors chasing Maddox and Bato was still in place. On our way, we'd felt a few aftershocks from the initial quake, and there was this tension in the air, like a bigger one was on its way.

Cal was the last to climb out of the well. We were anxious about bumping into the warriors in the hidden valley, but luck was on our side. Just as we got to the other side, the jungle went dead silent. No birds, no wind, just this spooky calm. Then it hit us—a massive earthquake. Doc later guessed it must've been at least a 7 on the

Richter scale. Boulders crashed down the mountainside, triggering landslides. We watched as the last standing megaliths toppled like dominos. Trying to stay upright was useless; we had to huddle at the base of a huge tree, praying it wouldn't crash down. When the shaking stopped, it felt surreal, like a pain suddenly gone. We slowly got back on our feet, relieved we'd made it through. But the landscape had changed—no megaliths left, and the entrance to the crystal cave and labyrinth was buried under a massive landslide.

As dust sprinkled down on us, Digger, taking off his hat and wiping his forehead, said, "Well, I don't think Tepanec survived that."

"Definitely not," Doc agreed.

I wrapped my arm around Atzi, knowing she'd be feeling a huge loss. "Everyone okay?" I checked.

"We're all good," Cal said. "But the real question is, how do we get back now?"

Grinning, Juno chimed in, "We walk due east. Sooner or later, we'll hit the Enchanted River."

And that's exactly what we did.

Sensing that Jax had concluded her tale, Janet leaned forward with curiosity. "So, what happened to Maddox and Bato?"

"Have no idea. For all we know, they made it to safety, or the warriors got them," Jax replied with a shrug.

"And it was just you, Doc, and Digger who made it back to Davao. What happened to the others?"

Jax sighed. "When we reached the Surigao River, we had no choice but to build rafts. It was a struggle, especially without proper tools. We ended up making three."

"Why three?" Janet asked, puzzled.

"Building one large enough for all of us was impossible, so Doc figured three rafts would be our best shot. Cal, Vehnee, and Dino took the first one; Digger, Doc, and I took the second; and Juno with Atzi had the last, which was the smallest. Initially, we tried to stay close, but on the second day, we hit rapids that separated us. By the time rescuers found us, we'd been drifting, famished and exhausted, for six days. I don't know if the others made it."

Janet's expression grew sombre. "Do you think anyone from Tepanec could have survived?"

Jax shook her head. "I doubt it. The photos Doc took show the extent of the devastation. If that cavern ceiling collapsed, it would've obliterated the city and everyone in it. A tragic end to what was an incredible, lost empire."

"Empire of the Lost," Janet mused. "Quite the fitting title. So, Jax de Loite, how does it feel to have been a queen, even if just for a day?"

Jax chuckled ruefully. "It just didn't sound right, Queen Jax ... and let's not even think about King Digger."

After the interview, Janet and Jax walked into Christina's office. As they settled opposite her desk, Christina leaned forward, handing Jax a small bag. Jax's face lit up with relief to see her phone and wallet—she had left them with Christina for safekeeping before the expedition.

"Happy with the interview?" Christina inquired.

"Yes, now I need to interview Doc and Digger," Janet replied.

Jax, looking anxious, interjected, "Have you heard from the hospital?"

Christina's smile was reassuring. "Yes, they've been discharged. I arranged for their transport here; they should arrive any moment. I was in the doorway listening to your story, Jax. It's unbelievable."

Jax chuckled lightly. "Gee, I hope not."

Christina looked puzzled. "What do you mean?"

Jax responded with a laugh, "Just joking. I want the audience to believe it."

As the door opened, Digger and Doc walked in. Jax leapt up, enveloping them in a warm embrace. Both men's faces were peeling from sunburn.

"You look like you could do with a good meal," Jax quipped.

It was true; they appeared gaunt. "I could eat a horse and chase the rider," Digger joked.

Doc's tone then turned sombre. "I've got some bad news, Jax." His grave voice dampened the mood. "My phone got wet on the raft and..."

"It's all lost?" Jax murmured, her voice barely above a whisper.

"Now it really is the lost empire," Janet added, her tone tinged with disappointment.

As Christina answered a phone call, a heavy silence enveloped the group, the weight of losing the crucial evidence hanging over them.

Doc apologised, "I tried to keep it safe, but the rapids ... It was impossible to keep dry."

"It's not the end of the world," Digger offered optimistically. "I've heard of cases where data is recovered from water-damaged phones."

Janet warned, "Yes, but it needs to be done like quickly."

Christina, finishing her call, re-joined them with a hopeful suggestion. "I know a data recovery specialist. He's very good, but it's a one-shot deal."

Janet's relief was palpable. "Fantastic, if we had to wait until Sydney it would've been all over red rover."

Christina shared more news, "That was Juno on the phone. He and Atzi are in Tula and doing fine."

The group's spirits lifted, especially Janet's. "An interview with Atzi would add so much credibility."

Christina's tone became serious. "I'm sorry, Janet, but that won't be possible."

Janet's confusion was evident. "Why not?"

Christina said warmly, "Janet, Atzi is the only known survivor of Tepanec and she carries the blood of the Aztecs. Atzi is and will be regarded a national treasure, her privacy is critical."

"I totally agree," Jax interrupted. "She has been through more than anyone can imagine, she can't be exposed until she has had time to assimilate in the 21st Century. Think of it, she virtually came from a community stuck in 16th Century ... all this would be mind-blowing for her ... car, planes, electricity, everything."

Digger agreed, "Too right, she needs time."

Christina elaborated, "She'll stay with the Santos family in Tula. The museum will support Atzi, Juno, and his family."

Jax, holding Christina's hand and with tears in her eyes, expressed her gratitude. "Thank you, Christina. She's a treasure."

"A world treasure," Doc added. "We have much to learn from her."

Digger chimed in, "Yes, she knows the story of our parents and Tepanec's history."

Christina concluded, "In time, we'll document her knowledge for the historical archives of the Philippines. We must be patient and careful in how we approach this."

Before leaving Mindanao, the group made their way to Tula to bid farewell. Captain Del Rosario hosted a reception at the police station. Juno's story had grown in the telling, and the locals now saw them as heroes. Jax was astonished at how quickly Atzi had adapted to modern life, now casually dressed in jeans and a Pink Floyd T-shirt. Yet, in a quiet moment away from Janet and her camera, the group shared a look that said it all—they had experienced something extraordinary together, an adventure that would forever bond them.

"I wonder if Maddox and Bato made it out?" Juno pondered aloud.

"They're survivors," Digger replied confidently. "I bet they'll show up eventually."

"Yeah, probably sooner than we think," Jax added.

"If they did make it," Christina interjected, "I'm sure I'll hear about a golden sceptre hitting the black market."

The group contemplated this, with Doc musing, "Could he really smuggle it out of the Philippines?"

Captain Del Rosario, overhearing them, joined in. "We're on it. Maddox won't be able to take the treasure out of Mindanao. We have eyes and ears everywhere, especially in the black market."

Juno chuckled. "What a character, that Maddox."

"He grabbed that staff and was off like a shot," Digger recalled with a laugh.

Saying goodbye to Atzi was emotional for Jax. The connection they shared was profound, almost spiritual. As they were parting, Jax asked her, "Do you miss your parents?"

Atzi revealed that her mother had passed when she was twelve and then she was cared for by Henry, Jax's father. Intrigued, Jax asked about her real father.

"Some say it was Ocelot, but it was a secret," Atzi replied.

"Why a secret?" Jax probed.

"Because of my mother."

Jax, puzzled, pressed further. Atzi's response left her speechless. "Your mother was Cindy?" Jax stammered.

Atzi's warm smile confirmed it. Jax was overwhelmed. Atzi, was her step-sister! It explained so much: why Henry had taken her in, taught her English, and why Coatl had chosen her for the sacrifice—she had royal blood, a threat to him.

Jax realised she had to ponder over this revelation and keep it from Janet and even Digger, to protect it from becoming part of The Next Files story. It wasn't until they were on the flight back to Sydney that she decided to share the truth with Digger.

The revelation that they now had another sister changed everything.

A week after returning to Sydney, Jax received a call to meet with Carter, who had news from Dr Jimenez. She made her way into his office, filled with a mix of anticipation and apprehension.

"Jax, how's the story coming along?" Carter inquired, as she pulled up a chair across from his desk.

"It's tough without Doc's photos … Did you…?" Jax began, her voice tinged with hope.

"Yes, Christina managed to recover some images from Doc's phone. No video, unfortunately, but we have four partials," Carter explained, turning his computer monitor to face her. The first image was a selfie of Jax, Doc, and Digger in front of a towering megalith.

"That's in the hidden valley," Jax recognised.

The next two images, although fragmented, depicted Jax's crowning by Coatl, but the detail was limited. The final photo, however, brought a beaming, tearful smile to Jax's face.

"That's Tepanec, as we first saw it from the cliff edge. I suppose this makes our story more believable?" she said, a hint of triumph in her voice.

"I never doubted you, Jax," Carter assured her, sharing in her excitement. "And here's a shot Christina took yesterday."

He showed her a selfie of Christina with Cal, Vehnee, and Dino. Tears welled up in Jax's eyes again. "They made it," she whispered, her relief obvious.

"Yep, and Tilly will be back in a few days. She's still helping Atzi adjust," Carter added.

Jax leaned back in her chair lost in thought. "I wonder if Maddox and Bato made it out?" she questioned aloud.

With the recovered photos, the amazing story of their adventure got a real visual hook, proving the wild ride they'd been on.

Catch the next adventure in **The Next Files** series:

BUNYIP

The song lyrics featured in this novel are with the permission of:
Keadybros Music Publishing

http://www.keadybros.com

'TAKE ME'
by Gary L. Keady
copyright©1997
performed by:
Allona
('Tomorrow on My Mind' album)

'SOMEWHERE IN MY MIND'
by Gary L. Keady & John M. Vallins
copyright©1997
performed by:
World
('At War with the Great Unknown' album)

visit:

https://www.bigislandpublishing.au

www.ingramcontent.com/pod-product-compliance
Lightning Source LLC
Chambersburg PA
CBHW020528120726
47904CB00003B/1003